David led Lena ▒▒▒▒▒

"Why don't you have ▒▒▒▒▒▒▒▒▒

She sat down slowly, staring at her hands.

"David?" she whispered. "If you all don't allow me to stay involved in this investigation, I'm afraid the killer will never be caught."

He sat down next to her and held her hand.

"I can understand why you feel that way. You're highly skilled at what you do. But we've got to keep you safe, Lena. Which means you can't keep anything from us. If you see something, you have to say something. Don't let your passion for your work get you killed. Deal?"

"Deal."

"And with that being said, I really think you should consider stepping away from the investigation. Take a break. Let the police handle the—"

"No," Lena interrupted. "I will not back down from this case, David."

He fell silent for several moments before responding.

"Understood."

The detective instinctively leaned down and kissed her softly on the forehead. She raised her head.

Their lips were inches apart...

THE HEART-SHAPED MURDERS

DENISE N. WHEATLEY

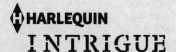

This book is dedicated to all of my fellow true crime junkies.
Keep sleuthing, friends!

HARLEQUIN®
INTRIGUE™

Recycling programs
for this product may
not exist in your area.

ISBN-13: 978-1-335-48966-1

The Heart-Shaped Murders

Copyright © 2022 by Denise N. Wheatley

For questions and comments about the quality of this book,
please contact us at CustomerService@Harlequin.com.

Harlequin Enterprises ULC
22 Adelaide St. West, 41st Floor
Toronto, Ontario M5H 4E3, Canada
www.Harlequin.com

Printed in U.S.A.

Denise N. Wheatley loves happy endings and the art of storytelling. Her novels run the romance gamut, and she strives to pen entertaining books that embody matters of the heart. She's an RWA member and holds a BA in English from the University of Illinois. When Denise isn't writing, she enjoys watching true crime TV and chatting with readers. Follow her on social media.

Instagram: @Denise_Wheatley_Writer
Twitter: @DeniseWheatley
BookBub: @DeniseNWheatley
Goodreads: Denise N. Wheatley

Books by Denise N. Wheatley

Harlequin Intrigue

Cold Case True Crime
Bayou Christmas Disappearance
The Heart-Shaped Murders

Visit the Author Profile page at Harlequin.com.

CAST OF CHARACTERS

Lena Love—A well-respected forensic investigator who works for the Los Angeles Police Department.

David Hudson—A devoted police detective who works for the police department of small-town Clemmington, California.

Kennedy Love—Clemmington's chief of police and Lena's strong-willed father.

Miles Love—Lena's younger brother, who serves as a Clemmington police officer. He's tough but also has a soft side.

Jake Love—Lena's stern older brother, who also serves as a Clemmington police officer and is known as his father's right-hand man.

Betty Love—Kennedy's wife and the matriarch of the Love family.

Russ Campbell—A Clemmington PD detective, known to be quite the ladies' man.

Lee Underwood—A kind, loyal Clemmington police officer.

Herschel Scott—The LAPD's chief of police and Lena's boss.

Chapter One

Lena Love kicked a rock out from underneath her foot, then bent down and tightened the twill shoelaces on her brown leather hiking boots.

The crime scene investigator, who doubled as a forensic science technician, stood back up and eyed Los Angeles' Cucamonga Wilderness trail. Sharp-edged stones and ragged shards of bark covered the rugged, winding terrain.

"Watch your step," she uttered to herself before continuing along the path of her latest crime scene.

Lena's eyes squinted as she focused on the trail. Heavy foliage loomed overhead, blocking out the sun's brilliant rays. She pulled out her flashlight, hoping its bright beam would help uncover potential evidence.

An ominous wave of vulnerability swept through her chest at the sight of the vast San Gabriel Mountains. She spun around slowly, feeling small while eyeing the infinite views of the forest, desert and snowy mountainous peaks.

The wild surroundings left her with a lingering sense of defenselessness. Lena tightened the belt on her tan suede blazer. She hoped it would give her some semblance of security.

It didn't.

Lena wondered if her latest victim felt that same vulnerability on the night she'd been brutally murdered.

"Come on, Grace Mitchell," Lena said aloud, as if the dead woman could hear her. "Talk to me. Tell me what happened to you. *Show* me what happened to you."

A gust of wind whipped Lena's bone-straight bob across her slender face. She tucked her hair behind her ears and stooped down, aiming the flashlight toward the majestic oak tree where Grace's body had been found.

Lena envisioned spotting droplets of blood, a cigarette butt, the tip of a latex glove…*anything* that would help identify the killer.

This was her second visit to the crime scene. The thought of showing up to the station without any viable evidence yet again caused an agonizing pang of dread to shoot up her spine.

Grace was the fifth victim of a criminal who Lena had labeled an organized serial killer. He appeared to have a type. Young, slender, brunette women. Their bodies had all been found in heavily wooded areas. Each victim's hands were meticulously tied behind their backs with a three-strand twisted rope. They'd been strangled to death. And the amount of evidence left at each scene was practically nonexistent.

But the killer's signature mark was always there. And it was a sinister one.

After murdering his victims, the predator would carve a heart into the chests of his victims with what looked to be a sharp blade.

"Ugh," Lena groaned, shivering at the gruesome thought of his actions.

The entire state of California, along with the victims' families and the media, had put an immense amount of pressure on the LAPD to catch the killer. As a result, Lena was recently assigned to the case.

The sound of a crackling tree branch stopped Lena dead in her tracks. She almost stumbled forward when the tips of her boots dipped into the dusty earth.

She quickly gathered herself and aimed her flashlight toward the noise. Bears and mountain lions were known to frequent the trail. So were hikers.

Unfortunately, so were serial killers.

Lena swallowed hard, questioning whether she should turn around and leave. But her resolve was stronger than both her fear and common sense combined.

"Maybe you just shouldn't have come out here alone…"

She did an abrupt 360-degree turn and waved her flashlight in the air. The stream of yellow light landed on several tree limbs that were swaying in the wind. Her shoulders relaxed a bit at the sight.

"See?" she said to herself. "It's nothing. You're good."

Lena chalked her panic up to paranoia and continued along the path.

"Come on, Grace," she whispered once again while shining her light along the edge of the trail. "Speak to me. Give me something to work with here."

Lena paused. She noticed what appeared to be two oddly shaped black lumps sticking out from underneath a tall shrub.

She stepped off the path and walked farther into the wooded area, then pressed the button on the back of her flashlight, increasing its brightness.

Are those lumps of coal? she asked herself while slowly moving in. *Remnants from a barbecue grill, maybe?*

But as Lena got closer, she realized that the lumps looked more like leather than sedimentary rocks.

"What the…?"

Lena dug around inside her pocket and pulled out a pair of latex gloves. She slipped them on, then bent down.

She pressed her fingertips against the black matter. It wasn't hard enough to be stone. But the smooth surface was firm.

She leaned farther into the brush. Shined her light down directly onto the objects. After a few moments, Lena realized that she was staring at a pair of black leather work boots.

"Bingo!" she exclaimed, thrilled to finally get her hands on a possible piece of evidence.

She reached down and grabbed the boots. But when

she tried to pick them up off the ground, they didn't budge.

"Come on," Lena grunted, wondering if the hot sun had caused the rubber soles to disintegrate into the dirt.

She pulled harder. The boots still did not move.

"*What* has these stuck?" Lena asked aloud.

The investigator gave the boots a firmer tug. Suddenly, one of them lifted off the ground. It kicked up so swiftly that it knocked her square in the forehead.

"*Ow!*" Lena yelled, falling backward onto the ground.

She closed her eyes and gripped her head. A bump was already beginning to form.

Lena slid her hands underneath her. The rocky soil scraped against her palms. She ignored the pain and brought her knees in close.

Just as she began to stand up, Lena was knocked back down again.

"*Dammit!*"

She was completely discombobulated. Strangely, the work boots she'd been trying to grab were now positioned directly in front of her.

Lena recoiled when they moved in closer. A shadowy figure hovered over her. Within a matter of seconds, she knew she was in danger.

Just as she opened her mouth to scream, a man pounced on Lena. She tried to kick him off, but his weight pinned her legs to the ground.

She tore at his arms. He overpowered her, his hands moving past her flailing limbs and going straight for her neck.

"No! Stop!" Lena attempted to yell. *"Help!"*

Her muffled screams were silenced by the howling wind. The attacker's hands were now wrapped firmly around her throat. Lena's voice was a mere whisper. Her vocal cords had been immobilized. And she was too deep into the woods to be seen from the trail.

This is it, she thought, tears falling from her eyes as the pressure behind them increased. *I cannot believe my life is going to end this way...*

Just when Lena felt herself losing consciousness, the predator loosened his grasp on her neck.

She gasped, choking on the huge puff of air that swept through her lungs. But before she could truly catch her breath, the attacker ripped open her blazer and tore at her blouse.

Pearlized buttons flew through the air. She emitted a guttural scream, punching her assailant in the chest.

He continued to overpower her. Lena's blows did nothing to deter his assault.

Your pepper spray, she thought. *Get to your pepper spray!*

She struggled to reach down inside the pocket of her black cargo pants. Just as she wrapped her fingers around the canister, Lena felt a cold, sharp blade slice into her skin.

Her mouth fell open. But nothing came out. She was too stunned to make a sound.

This can't be happening. This can't be happening!

The blade continued to carve into her chest. That's when it struck Lena. She was being attacked by the serial killer she'd been pursuing.

You will not be his sixth victim, Lena told herself. *Fight back. Fight!*

Burning pain tore through her chest. She bit down on her bottom lip and snatched the pepper spray from her pocket. Lena held the canister directly in front of his masked face, closed her eyes and hit the red button.

"Aah!" he grunted.

As the man howled in pain, Lena opened her eyes slightly.

He was up on his knees, still hovering over her while covering his face with his gloved hands.

She quickly jumped up and kneed him in the groin. His screams caught in his throat. A hissing wheeze oozed through his mask.

When he rolled over and curled up into the fetal position, Lena took advantage of the moment. She jumped up and hurried back toward the trail, tearing down the pathway toward the canyon's entrance.

Lena wanted to turn around to see if her attacker was following her. But she was too afraid of losing her footing. So she kept moving forward.

She could feel the blood pouring from her chest. The chilled mountain air stung the open wound. But the gash was the least of her concerns. All Lena cared about was reaching her car and getting the hell out of there.

As the trail began to open up, she heard faint footsteps pounding behind her.

Just keep going, she told herself. *Keep going!*

After what seemed like forever, Lena finally reached the parking lot. It was practically empty.

Her wide eyes darted anxiously. A surge of relief eased the terror running through her limbs when her silver Jeep came into view.

Lena charged toward the vehicle. But as it got closer, sharp cramps began to shoot up her legs.

Don't you dare stop now, her inner voice screamed as the sound of looming footsteps persisted. *Keep going!*

She fought through the pain and forced herself to run faster. Lena grabbed her keys from her back pocket, pounding the fob until the button unlocked the doors.

She reached the car door, then turned around. A shadowy figure appeared at the parking lot's entrance.

It was her attacker.

He quickly limped toward her, holding his groin with one hand while swiping his eyes with the other.

Lena emitted a short, panicked scream.

"Get back here, you *bitch*!" he yelled.

She inhaled sharply. Her fingers trembled as she grabbed the handle and threw open the door.

His heavy footsteps were drawing nearer. Her assailant was getting closer.

"Aw, is she *scared*?" he taunted. "Did you actually think you were gonna catch me? It'll never happen, sweetheart. But I caught *you*. And after I finish what I started on that delicate little chest of yours, I'm gonna kill you!"

"Stay away from me!" Lena tried to shout. But her voice sounded more like a whimper than a command.

The cramps in her legs intensified as she struggled to climb inside the Jeep. She grabbed the side of the driver's seat and pulled herself up.

Finally, she was in.

Lena's chest heaved with panic. She pressed down on the brake and frantically pushed the start button. The door hadn't closed all the way before she threw the gearshift into Drive.

Her attacker was only a few feet away. He ran toward the front of her Jeep, still holding his groin. She looked into his pale gray eyes. There was something oddly familiar behind their cold, menacing glare.

One thing was for certain. He appeared determined to take her out. And judging by the blood that continued to seep from her chest, he'd almost completed his mission.

Lena rammed her right foot down onto the accelerator. She slammed her door shut, then tore through the parking lot.

She craned her neck, blinking back tears while glancing in the rearview mirror. Lena watched in horror as her attacker jumped inside a black sports car. Its huge spiked chrome wheels screeched loudly as he sped after her.

Lena's chest tightened. Thin streams of air barely filled her lungs. She whipped her Jeep around the mountain's sharp turns, all while struggling to catch a glimpse of her assailant's license plate. It was obscured by a black shield.

Stay calm. Just get to the hospital. Stay calm. Just get to the hospital, Lena kept telling herself.

When she reached the bottom of the mountain, Lena made a quick right turn onto a desolate road. She pulled behind a large dumpster, making sure her Jeep was hidden from the main street.

The sound of her attacker's roaring engine filled the air. Lena's eyes were glued to the side-view mirror.

Please keep going. Please keep going, she repeated over and over again.

Her prayers were answered when the car flew past the side road.

Lena's chest heaved with relief. She waited several minutes before spinning around and creeping toward the main street. It was clear. She sped off toward the hospital.

When she pulled into the emergency room's lot, Lena opened the console and pulled out a stack of napkins. She pressed them against her wound. Blood quickly soaked into the stark white paper, turning it into a bright shade of crimson. The sight, along with the intense pain, caused her to cry out in agony.

She pulled down the sun visor and slid open the mirror.

Lena stared at the wound on her chest. She studied the curved, half-cordate symbol.

After I finish what I started on that delicate little chest of yours, I'm gonna kill you!

The attacker's words echoed through her mind. The

half-shaped heart he'd carved into her skin would be a permanent reminder that she was almost murdered by her most elusive suspect to date.

And now, it was a race against time to catch him before he really did finish what he'd started.

Chapter Two

"Ouch," Detective David Hudson hissed after a splash of hot coffee spilled from his cup and singed his hand.

"Gotta wait for it to cool off, hon," Milly called out from the police station's front desk. "I just brewed that pot about ten seconds ago."

The receptionist, who doubled as the 9-1-1 operator, didn't miss much that went on around the station. Or their entire town of Clemmington, California, for that matter.

"Yes, ma'am," David uttered through clenched teeth. He waved his hand in the air, hoping that would help ease the sting.

"Why don't you grab a few ice cubes out of the freezer?" Milly suggested, staring at the handsome detective from the corner of her eye while fluffing her tightly curled silver bouffant hairdo. "Apply them to your burn so you won't get a blister. I can help you if you want…"

"Stop flirting, Milly!" Detective Russ Campbell yelled out from his office. "Hudson's young enough to be your grandson!"

"I'd say that's pushin' it, Campbell!" Milly growled. "Oh, and by the way, mind your business! Nobody out here is talking to you."

"If it's within earshot, then it *is* my business!" Russ barked back.

David chuckled at the bickering twosome. They seemed to get entangled in some sort of altercation at least three times a day.

"Thanks for the advice, Milly," David said, extending his muscular arm and giving her an affectionate fist bump.

Milly pulled her fist away from his and emitted an explosion sound effect through her puckered ruby-red lips. She then wiggled her stubby fingers, which were adorned with vintage gold rings and long acrylic French tips.

"You're welcome, sweetheart," she murmured. "It's good to know *somebody* appreciates me around here."

"We all appreciate you," he assured her.

David then turned around and headed back to his office.

On the way there, he could feel Milly's piercing green eyes watching him as he walked away. David was used to that sort of attention by now and didn't give it much thought.

For years, the detective's fellow townspeople tried to talk him into leaving small-town Clemmington behind and heading to Hollywood. They were convinced that his dark, deep-set eyes, smooth cocoa-brown complexion, lush lips and athletic build would garner a lucrative career in the entertainment business.

But David, who downplayed his rugged good looks, found nothing appealing about being in the limelight. He was fully dedicated to life in his hometown and work in criminal justice.

David entered his small, modest office and closed the door. He walked past an old silver filing cabinet and slammed his fist against the top drawer. Per usual, it popped right back open thanks to all the dog-eared files stuffed inside.

David pulled his well-worn black mesh ergonomic chair out from under the rustic cherrywood desk. He sat down slowly, clenching his jaws as pain shot up his thighs. Yesterday was leg day at the gym and his quads had yet to recover.

Just as he took a sip of coffee, which had finally cooled down, David heard a knock at the door. Before he could say anything, it slowly opened.

He looked up and saw Miles Love, one of Clemmington's most well-respected police officers, standing in the doorway.

"Hey, Dave, you got a sec?"

"Yeah, of course, man. Come on in."

David's eyelids lowered as he watched the officer saunter inside the office. Miles was usually cheerful, but today his face appeared twisted with worry.

"What's with the long face?" David asked him. "You having woman problems again?"

"I wish that was the problem…"

Miles slid his hands inside the pockets of his black uniform pants, blinking rapidly while staring down at the floor.

David pointed at the chair across from his desk. "Do you wanna have a seat and talk about whatever it is that's bothering you?"

Miles shook his head from side to side without looking up.

David's concern grew. A feeling of dread overcame him as he watched the color in Miles's reddish-brown complexion drain from his face.

"Nah," Miles mumbled. "I'd rather keep standing. I, uh—I guess you haven't checked the breaking news alerts on your cell phone lately."

"No, not recently." David grabbed his phone and punched in the security code. "Why? Did I miss something?"

Miles looked up at the ceiling, his chest now heaving as though he were having a panic attack. "It's Lena. She, um…" He paused, his gravelly voice cracking underneath the weight of his words. "She's been attacked."

David froze. His cell phone slipped out of his hand, thumping loudly when it slammed against the desk. "She's been *what*?"

"She's been attacked," Miles repeated.

"When did this happen?" David asked, struggling to remain calm for the sake of Miles, considering Lena was his sister. "*How* did this happen? And do they know who did it?"

"It happened yesterday. Lena was alone, investigating a crime scene when she was assaulted. The LAPD thinks it was done by the serial killer they've been pursuing. So does she." Miles paused. He dropped his head in his hands and pressed his fingertips against the corners of his damp eyes. "That—that *animal*..."

"I'm so sorry, man," David whispered.

The detective swallowed hard in an attempt to keep down the mix of pain and guilt creeping up his throat. He ran his hand down his goatee, his mind racing in a million different directions.

"Wait," David said, looking back up at Miles. "If the attack happened yesterday, why are you just now finding out about it?"

Miles shrugged before emitting a deep sigh. "Lena said she didn't want to worry the family before getting herself checked out at the hospital. Honestly, I think it's a pride thing. You know how she is. My baby sis can't stand the thought of failing at something or making a misstep."

"Humph, don't I know it. So you had to find out about this through the media?"

"Yep. Unfortunately."

"That woman..." David writhed his hands together, hoping that the pressure would somehow purge the frustration stirring inside his body. Hearing Miles speak of Lena's stubbornness triggered thoughts from their past.

David and Lena had been high school sweethearts. They were deeply in love. But that love wasn't strong enough to keep her in Clemmington.

They'd always planned on attending the local college and building a life together in their hometown. But during their senior year, Lena decided that she wanted to attend southern California's Pacific Western University and enroll in the school's prestigious forensic science program.

David was disappointed but confident they could maintain a long-distance relationship during those four years. However, when Lena informed him that she planned on moving to LA after graduation and working for the LAPD, that confidence faded.

He was shocked by the news that Lena didn't want to return to Clemmington. Aside from their relationship, David assumed she would want to work for their hometown's police department since her father served as the chief of police, and both of her brothers were police officers. But he'd been wrong.

Lena craved the excitement of working in a big city and welcomed the challenges of LA's multifaceted criminal investigations. When David expressed his desire to remain loyal to Clemmington, the pair acrimoniously parted ways.

After Lena moved away for good, David was left feeling abandoned. And now, he was regretful. Because had she stayed by his side, she never would've been attacked.

Miles cleared his throat and slowly backed out of the doorway. "I'd better get to my parents' house and check on my mother. Can you hold things down until I get back? My father and brother already left for LA to pick Lena up and bring her back here."

David shot straight up in his chair. "Wait, Lena's coming here? To Clemmington?"

"Yes. She's too traumatized to stay in LA. So she's gonna take a leave of absence and come home for a while and recuperate. But I don't know…"

David looked on curiously as Miles ran his hand down his beard, his voice trailing off. "You don't know what?"

"I'm just wondering how things are gonna go when Lena gets to town. She wasn't on the best of terms with my family when she left Clemmington. We all felt betrayed after she chose to work for the LAPD instead of our police department."

David felt a pull inside his chest after hearing those words spoken aloud. Apparently, he wasn't the only one still affected by Lena's departure.

"You know," David began, "nobody was more disappointed when she moved away than me. But at this point, that's all irrelevant. We've got to put our differences aside and make sure she's okay."

"Oh, I agree with you one hundred percent. But are *you* gonna be able to do that after everything you two have been through?"

The lawmen stared one another down. David was surprised that Miles had brought up the couple's tumultuous past. But Miles was well aware of their unresolved issues that they never addressed before Lena left town.

"Of course I'll be able to do that," David insisted. "I can't bring our personal issues into this situation. Right now, my only concern is Lena's well-being."

"Yeah, okay. We'll see…" Miles replied, his low

tone dripping with skepticism. "I'd better get to my parents' house. I'll be back later this afternoon."

"Please send Mrs. Love my regards. Tell her I'm thinking of her and the family."

"It would be nice if you stopped by and told her that yourself. I'm sure she's expecting to see you once Lena gets home."

David stared blankly at Miles. A pang of uncertainty thumped inside his gut. As concerned as he was about Lena, he wasn't ready to see her just yet.

"I'll give you an update on things when I get back," Miles continued without waiting for a response, as if sensing the pressure in David's hesitation. "Call or text me if anything goes down. Not that things ever do in this town."

"Will do. Thanks for keeping me in the loop."

"No problem."

The minute Miles left his office, David turned to his computer. Despite his coffee now being lukewarm, he took a long sip, then pulled up the *Los Angeles Times*' website.

There it was. The top story, flashing across the screen.

Famed Crime Scene Investigator Lena Love Attacked by California Serial Killer!

David's stomach flipped as he gazed at the beautiful photo of Lena that accompanied the story.

Do not start with that, he told himself before turning his attention to the article.

As he studied the details surrounding Lena's attack, any ill feelings David held toward her slowly dissipated. They were replaced by the sudden desire to protect her.

Chapter Three

Lena sat at her parents' dining room table, her hands clenched together tightly. She couldn't seem to control her jittery knees as they bounced against the sharp oak edge.

"Here you go, honey," Lena's mother, Betty, said. She set a cup of chamomile tea in front of her. "Be careful. It's hot."

"Thanks, Mom."

The sting of guilt singed Lena's skin when she looked up at her. The skin underneath Betty's swollen eyes was a pale shade of burgundy. Lines of worry ran down her quivering chin. Her wavy, salt-and-pepper hair was pulled back into a disheveled ponytail.

Betty placed her hand on Lena's back and began massaging it, just like she used to do when Lena couldn't sleep as a child.

Lena closed her eyes and exhaled. After several moments, her mother stopped abruptly. When she opened her eyes, Betty was hurrying over to the curio cabinet.

She threw open the doors and began pulling out glasses, then vigorously wiping them down. Lena

wanted to ask if she was okay, especially considering the glasses were already gleaming. But she didn't.
She realized that her mother was trying to keep busy
in hopes of calming her frazzled nerves.

Lena picked up her white porcelain teacup and blew
on the steaming liquid, then focused on the wall in
front of her.

A portrait of the family hung in the middle. It had
been taken right after Lena's college graduation, before she'd broke the news that she planned on moving
to Los Angeles and working for the LAPD.

Everyone looked so happy in the picture. But shortly
after the photo shoot, nothing was the same. Things
had been strained between them to say the least, which
was why Lena hadn't been back to Clemmington to
visit in several years.

She turned away from the picture and glanced
around her parents' spacious, ranch-style house. The
sight brought tears to Lena's eyes. Her mother, who
was a retired elementary school teacher, had main-
tained the home beautifully. It's where Lena and her
brothers grew up, and not much had changed since
she'd moved away.

The family room's neutral color scheme and rustic
decor brought back memories of game nights and get-
togethers among their classmates. The pang of nostalgia caused Lena to realize just how much she missed
those nights, along with her parents and siblings. It also
made her wonder whether leaving had been a mistake.

Just as her mind drifted toward thoughts of the at-

tack, Lena's father, Kennedy, and brother Jake saun-
tered into the dining room.

The Love men looked as though they could've been
triplets. They were each slightly over six feet tall, with
muscular builds and strong, refined features. The only
traits that set them apart were Kennedy's bald head
and thick mustache.

"Dad and I threw together some turkey sandwiches," Jake said to Lena, placing a platter filled with
mini hoagies in the middle of the table. "We, uh, we
figured you may be hungry."

"Thanks, Jay. I appreciate that," Lena told him, even
though she had no appetite. Eating was the last thing
on her mind.

Her father remained silent while pulling a cream-
colored chair away from the table. He sighed deeply,
sitting down slowly while running his fingertips across
his forehead's frown lines.

Lena felt herself growing sick at the thought of
stressing her family to this extent. It was the reason she
didn't initially tell them about the attack. Between their
tense exchanges and the trauma of being assaulted, she
was tempted to pack up and go back to LA.

Her rigid muscles relaxed a bit when Miles came
strolling into the room. He was the only one in the
family who'd stayed in regular contact with her after
she moved away.

"I'd better go check on the pot roast," Betty muttered before rushing toward the kitchen.

Lena shifted in her seat and looked up at Miles.

When he walked over to her chair, she noticed a silver flask discreetly tucked in his hand.

"What is that you have?" she whispered.

"Whiskey. Have some. It'll help calm your nerves."

Lena glanced over at her father and Jake, who were both busy digging into the sandwich platter. Sitting in her parents' home made her feel as though she shouldn't be drinking alcohol, despite being way past the legal age.

"A shot of whiskey is exactly what I need right now," she told Miles. "Hit me."

As he poured the brown liquor into her cup, the doorbell rang.

Lena jumped in her chair, still on edge after being attacked.

"Relax," Miles said. He gently placed his hand on her shoulder. "You're good. That's probably David."

"David!" Lena exclaimed, her eyes widening. "What is he doing here?"

"He wanted to come by and check on you. Make sure you're okay. Why don't you go get the door while I go into the kitchen and check on Mom?"

"Wait, no. I don't want to. Why can't you—"

Before Lena could finish, Miles gave her a sly grin, then turned around and left the room.

She turned to her father and Jake, who were staring down at their plates. Lena couldn't help but think they were focusing on their food in an effort to avoid talking to her.

Aside from asking if she was okay a few times on the drive from LA to Clemmington, the ride had pretty much been silent. She knew they felt badly about the attack and didn't want to drill her. But Lena also realized that hurt feelings still lingered within the family over her move.

The doorbell rang again.

"You've gotta face him at some point," Lena's father said quietly. "Regardless of what went on in your past, David does still care about you. So go on. Answer the door."

Lena wanted to roll her eyes. But instead she nodded her head and slowly slid her chair away from the table. Before standing up, she took a long sip of her spiked tea.

"Is somebody going to get the door?" Betty called out from the kitchen.

"I'm getting it now!" Lena replied.

"Don't be scared," Jake snorted.

"Oh, stop it," she shot back, swiping his shoulder. When he gave her a smirk and a wink, Lena couldn't help but appreciate the snarky gesture.

Maybe the icy atmosphere is starting to melt... she thought.

"Stop teasing your sister," Kennedy said.

"Thank you, Daddy."

Lena took her time heading to the door. On the way there, she stopped in front of the mirror hanging on the living room wall and ran her fingers through her hair.

What are you doing? she asked herself, waving her hand at her reflection.

The doorbell rang a third time.

"I got it!" she called out before any of her family members could say a word.

Lena took a deep breath. She tucked her fitted white blouse into her dark blue jeans, then finally opened the door.

The sight of David almost knocked her down. She hadn't seen him since she'd left Clemmington. He certainly hadn't looked this clean-cut, fit and handsome before her departure.

"Hello, Lena," he said, his smooth voice flowing like Dennis Haysbert's in an Allstate commercial. "It's, uh, it's good to see you."

"Hi. It's—it's good to see you, too."

David handed her a bouquet of yellow roses. "I hope these'll help lift your spirits a bit."

"You remembered," she murmured, holding the bouquet to her nose and inhaling its sweet, fruity aroma. "Thank you."

"Of course I remembered. How could I ever forget your favorite flower?"

The pair gazed quietly at one another for several moments. A slight tingling began to flow through Lena's body.

What in the hell is going on? she asked herself. The last thing she'd expected was to feel this way upon seeing David.

The spell was broken when her mother entered the living room.

"David," Betty said, "thank you so much for coming over. Come on inside. Can I get you something to drink?"

"Oh no, Mrs. Love," he said, stepping across the threshold. "I'm fine. I just wanted stop by and check on everyone. And of course see how Lena is doing."

As he entered the house, David's muscular forearm brushed up against Lena's arm. She took a deep breath and stepped back.

When he paused and glanced over at her, the scent of his woodsy, aquatic cologne filled her nostrils. That tingling she'd been feeling transformed into full-blown pulsations.

"Are you okay?" he asked.

Lena could've sworn she heard a tinge of amusement in his voice. "Yep. I'm fine."

Betty approached David and gave him a warm hug. "Well, we really appreciate you stopping by to check on us. I'll leave you two alone so you can talk. Plus I need to get back to my pot roast. David, why don't you stay for dinner?"

He hesitated, then turned to Lena.

When David raised his eyebrows, she realized that he was silently asking for her permission. She nodded her head.

"Thank you, Mrs. Love," David replied. "I'd love to stay for dinner. As long as it's all right with Lena."

"Of course it is," she responded a bit quicker than she'd intended. "I—I mean, yeah, that's fine."

"Good," Betty said. "I'd better go and get those sandwiches off the dining room table before your father and brothers ruin their appetites. And here," she continued, taking the bouquet of flowers from Lena, "I'll put these beautiful roses in water for you."

"Thanks, Mom."

Betty paused, her eyes darting back and forth between Lena and David. The huge grin on her face said more than words ever could.

"Thanks, Mom," Lena repeated, through clenched teeth this time.

Betty caught the hint and hurried out of the room.

Lena turned to David and chuckled lightly, embarrassed by her mother's behavior.

"Sorry about that," she said before pointing over at the couch. "Why don't we have a seat. Are you sure you don't want anything to drink? Soda? Tea? Water?"

"No, I'm good. I think I drank about three pots of coffee today. But thank you."

Lena led the way as she and David sat down on the beige sectional sofa. She kept a safe distance, considering she was still waiting for the body tingles to stop. When she noticed David staring at her intently, Lena glanced around the room in search of something to say. The last thing she wanted to discuss was her attack.

"I have to tell you something," she blurted out.

"What's that?"

"I was drinking chamomile tea spiked with whiskey before you got here."

"Oh no. Not you. I can't even see Miss Top Shelf Wine and Champagne drinking whiskey."

"Yeah, but I was. After everything I've been through? I needed it. Blame Miles. He's the one that gave it to me."

"Ugh," David groaned, throwing his head back. "Here you go. Blaming one of your brothers for your wild behavior, per usual. I see not much has changed around the Love residence."

"And as long as I can keep getting away with it, things never will."

Lena was surprised by how relaxed she felt with David. Despite their complicated past, it was as if no time had passed between them.

She looked up at him. There was a pained look behind his eyes. She was suddenly hit with a bout of remorse.

Lena knew David was still hurt over the way she'd left Clemmington. But it wasn't just that. She could sense that he was upset by her assault.

"So, on a serious note," he said, "how are you doing?"

Lena's eyes fell to her lap. The high energy in the room shifted. It was replaced by a heavy gloom. She was quickly reminded of why she was back in Clemmington.

The moment when Lena's attacker knocked her to the ground flashed through her mind.

Stop it, she told herself, shaking her head in an attempt to erase the memory.

"I'm hanging in there. I mean, of course I'm still shaken up." She paused, curling her trembling hands into tight fists. "I just can't believe what happened at that crime scene. How did *I* end up getting assaulted by the killer that I'm pursuing, and almost killed, and…"

When Lena's voice trailed off, David slid in closer toward her.

"Are you sure it's the same suspect you've been

after?" he asked. "Or could it have been a random attack?"

Lena cleared her throat, swallowing a lump of nausea. She held her hand to her chest. Her fingers pressed against the thick bandage covering the scar underneath her blouse. That half-heart-shaped wound was a clear indication that her attacker was their serial killer.

The LAPD hadn't revealed the particulars of her assault to the media, specifically the details surrounding her scar. And in that moment, Lena wasn't ready to share them with David, either.

"It definitely wasn't a random attack," she told him. "City officials are feeling an intense amount of pressure to solve this case now that a fifth victim has been found. The mayor held a press conference a few weeks ago and introduced me as the newest member of the investigative team. After mentioning a couple of high-profile cases that I helped solve, I vowed to find the killer. *That's* why he's after me."

"So you think he trailed you to this latest crime scene you've been investigating?"

"I do. He was probably staking out the forensics lab. That's where I was before heading to the Cucamonga Wilderness trail."

David shook his head. "I don't like the way LA's city officials are handling this situation. At all."

"What do you mean?"

"That press conference put you in a very precarious position. We do things differently in Clemmington. We protect our own. Our police department never would've shined a public spotlight on you like that."

"Yeah, that probably wasn't the smartest thing to do," Lena muttered, wincing as she rubbed the back of her neck.

"Are you okay?"

"I'm fine," she replied, once again leaving out the details of the half-shaped heart that had been carved into her chest.

"Good. I'm glad you're back in Clemmington, Lena. I hope you'll stay for a while. Lay low and allow yourself some time to heal. What you experienced was extremely traumatizing. Maybe you should even consider letting another forensic investigator take over the case while you focus on your recovery."

Lena leaned into the back of the couch. "Humph. I don't know about all that. It sounds like the right thing to do. But honestly, I don't know how long I can just sit still. And I definitely can't see myself letting the case go. I've been investigating this killer for a few weeks, and I'm too close to cracking it to turn back now."

David stared at her, his steely eyes defiant.

"Your ambition always did override any advice I could ever give you," he said.

"I just like to finish what I start. That's all."

"Except when it comes to us," David shot back just as Betty walked back into the room.

"You two ready for dinner?" she asked cheerily.

"I am," Lena replied, quickly hopping up from the couch and heading to the dining room. It was bad enough that David had popped up at the house unexpectedly. The last thing she was prepared to do was hash out their unresolved issues.

He stood up and followed closely behind her. She could feel his intense gaze on her back.

"This conversation isn't over," he murmured.

What have I gotten myself into with this trip back to Clemmington...?

Chapter Four

David strolled into the police station and headed straight to the breakroom to grab a cup of coffee.

"Good morning, Detective Hudson," Milly sang out. "Looks like you've got a little extra pep in your step today."

"Do I?" he asked curiously.

But David knew exactly what Milly was referring to. Ever since Lena had come home, there was a rousing energy flowing through him that he couldn't seem to contain.

"Yes," Milly replied, propping her elbows on the edge of her cluttered desk and clicking her nails together. "You do. I wonder if it has anything to do with what's going on inside Chief Love's office."

David's eyebrows furrowed with confusion. He almost asked her to elaborate before realizing he didn't have time. He needed to check in with the chief on an act of vandalism that occurred earlier that morning across town.

"We're going to have to reconvene on whatever it is

you're referring to," he told her. "I've got a few things I need to take care of."

"Suit yourself," Milly told him. She flipped through a stack of reports and began sliding them inside manila folders. "In the meantime, I hope you guys catch whoever defaced the front of Mr. Young's beautiful art gallery."

"I'm sure we will."

David entered the breakroom and acknowledged the few police officers who were gathered around one of several white folding tables. They nodded their heads to him, then turned their attention back to a video they were watching on Officer Lee Underwood's cell phone.

After pouring himself a cup of coffee, David glanced down at his watch. It was already after nine o'clock.

Put a move on, he told himself, holding his cup steady while rushing to his office.

He tossed his briefcase down onto the desk and grabbed a notebook, then headed to Chief Love's office.

"Come on in, Detective," the chief said. "Have a seat. I hope it's okay that Lena is here. She was getting antsy sitting in the house all day. So she came down to the station to keep her dear old dad company."

"And once again get grilled on why I left Clemmington," Lena interjected. "Don't forget to add *that* little detail."

"Hey, if you wanna hang out with the boss, then you have to deal with the trash talk. It comes with the territory."

David chuckled at their friendly father-daughter banter. He was pleasantly surprised to see the pair getting along so well considering they were discussing such a touchy subject.

Lena turned to David and threw her hands in the air. "I cannot believe that after all this time, my father and brothers are *still* salty that I moved to LA."

"Your family just misses you, that's all. Take it as a compliment."

"I bet we're not the only ones who've missed her…" Chief Love said.

David's eyes lowered as he noticed a smirk on the chief's face.

Just let it go and sit down, David told himself before taking a seat next to Lena.

"*Anyway*," David said, "should we go ahead and get this meeting started?"

"Yes, we should," Chief Love replied.

While the chief flipped through his planner, David glanced over at Lena. That rousing energy he'd been feeling intensified as he discreetly studied her.

She was dressed casually in a fitted denim jumpsuit and white sneakers. Her hair had been pulled up into a messy bun, and her glowing skin appeared makeup free. Only a sheer coat of gloss covered her full lips. She looked relaxed, and absolutely beautiful.

"But before we get started," Chief Love said, "I've gotta get in one last word."

"Uh-oh," Lena mumbled, slumping down in her chair. "Here we go…"

"Lena," he continued, "you come from a family

of law enforcement officers. We run Clemmington, California. Why would you have ever wanted to ruin the family legacy?"

She leaned forward, gripping the arms on her chair. "I cannot believe you want to talk about this right now. Seriously, can I just recuperate in peace?"

Lena turned to David as if waiting on him to chime in.

He stared down at his notebook, not wanting to get in between the father and daughter. Not only that, but he needed to focus on something other than her stunning face.

"I plead the Fifth," David told her. "My arms are too short to box with the Love family."

"Oh, come on, Dave!" Chief Love insisted. "You may have dated my daughter back in the day, but you're *my* guy. You should be on my side."

"I'm on Sweden's side," he joked before flipping to a blank page in his notebook. "Now, what's going on with this act of vandalism? Milly mentioned that someone defaced Mr. Young's art gallery?"

"Yes, that's what it looks like." The chief slid several pieces of paper across the desk. "I had Jake and Miles drive by there earlier, assess the scene and take these photos."

David leaned forward, studying the pictures. The words *One Two I Am Coming For You* had been spray-painted in black across the gallery's storefront glass.

"Hmm, that's strange," David said. "What time did this happen?"

"According to Mr. Young's security cameras, around three o'clock this morning."

"Were the cameras able to capture a decent image of the perp?"

The chief leaned back in his chair and propped his hands on top of his head.

"Not really. All Mr. Young could gather was that the offender appeared to be male. He was dressed in what looked to be dark green camouflage hunting gear and a full tactical face mask. I'm surprised he went to such great lengths just to vandalize a storefront."

"Why don't I go by the gallery and take a look around?" David suggested as he jotted down notes. "I'll see what I can find and hopefully take a look at those surveillance tapes."

"That sounds good," Chief Love said. "Hopefully you can question Mr. Young and find out who he thinks may have done this. When Jake and Miles went by there earlier, he was too upset to speak with them."

Lena picked up one of the photos and studied it intently. "Poor Mr. Young. He's so sweet and doesn't bother anybody. And his art gallery means everything to him. He takes so much pride in it. I can't imagine who'd want to do something like this."

David picked up the other photos and eyed each of them again. "'One two I am coming for you...'" he read aloud before looking up at the chief. "Maybe this message wasn't aimed at Mr. Young."

"What do you mean?" Chief Love asked.

"Well, for starters, I agree with Lena. Mr. Young is a beloved member of this community. And even though he was upset when Jake and Miles stopped by, if he had a clue as to who would have done something like this, he would've reported it."

"I'd like to think so," the chief replied. "But where are you going with this?"

"The art gallery is located in one of the most visible areas in town. Maybe the perpetrator just wanted to leave this message somewhere he knew it would be seen in hopes that his target would receive it."

As soon as the words were out of David's mouth, his stomach dropped.

This message may have been left for Lena...

He glanced over at her, hoping she wasn't thinking what he was thinking. She was still staring down at one of the photos, seemingly oblivious.

David then looked up at the chief. He too was studying one of the pictures, rubbing his chin curiously. David couldn't tell whether he and his boss were on the same page or not. If they were, Chief Love wasn't letting on.

"I'm gonna head over to the gallery now," David said, slamming his notebook shut and hopping up. He was irritated with himself for almost saying too much. Lena had already been through enough. The last thing he wanted to do was cause any alarm, especially if his suspicions didn't hold much merit.

"Hey," Lena said, grabbing his arm, "is it okay if I ride with you? I'd love to take a look at the scene, too."

David stared down at her. There was a hunger in her intent gaze. The look was a reminder of how much she loved her work.

David turned to his boss. Chief Love shrugged his shoulders and scooted away from the desk.

"Well," the chief began, "Lena is a crime scene expert. You never know what she may find. And she had a great relationship with Mr. Young back when she still lived in Clemmington. She and her brothers actually used to volunteer at the gallery whenever he had openings. So it may not be a bad idea for her to ride along."

Lena pointed at her father. "Exactly. Plus, if I don't get back to some semblance of my normal life, I just may lose my mind."

David looked on apprehensively as she stood up and grabbed her purse.

"Are you sure you're ready for this?" he asked her. "You know…after what you've been through?"

"Listen, Detective Hudson," Lena said, brushing past him and pausing in the doorway, "I am a pro. This is what I do. And it's just an act of vandalism. It would be different if you were investigating a murder scene. Trust me. I can handle this. Now, let's hurry up and get to the gallery before Mr. Young calls a cleaning service to have the graffiti removed."

David paused, giving the chief one last time to talk his daughter down.

"You heard the lady," Chief Love quipped. "You'd better put a move on before Mr. Young compromises the crime scene."

"Thanks, boss," Lena said to her father.

She spun around and strutted out of the office. David followed behind her, fighting off a mix of frustration and excitement.

Milly perked up when the pair walked past her desk. "Where are you two off to?"

David's eyes shifted at the suggestive tone in her high-pitched voice.

"We're going to check out the crime scene at Mr. Young's art gallery," he told her.

"*Ohhh.* And Miss Lena Love is joining you?"

"Yes, I am," Lena replied. "It's time for me to get back into the swing of things. Even if it is with the Clemmington PD as opposed to the LAPD."

"*Please,*" Milly snorted, the red beads on her bracelets jingling loudly as she waved Lena off. "The LAPD ain't got nothing on us."

"If you say so," Lena retorted.

"But seriously, hon, I'm glad to see you're doing okay," Milly said before giving her a sympathetic smile. "You had this entire town worried for a minute there."

"Thanks, Mills. I know a lot of the townspeople were pretty disappointed when I moved away. So hearing that means a lot."

David gently placed his hand on Lena's shoulder.

"We'd better get going. Milly, we'll be back in a bit. Call my cell phone if anyone needs me."

"I most certainly will, Detective. *Byyye* you two."

He threw her a look as she grinned and wiggled her fingers at the pair.

The people of Clemmington may have held a grudge toward Lena when she'd left town. But they certainly seemed to have softened up quickly now that she had returned.

Including you... David told himself.

As soon as the thought crossed his mind, he pushed it aside. He'd already gotten hurt once when she moved away. And he knew she'd be returning to LA eventually.

So don't fall for her again...

Chapter Five

A burst of adrenaline flowed through Lena's veins when David pulled up in front of Mr. Young's art gallery.

The building stood prominently on the corner of Clemmington's busiest downtown strip. Its contemporary glass exterior was a stark contradiction to the surrounding brick storefronts.

Today, however, the gallery appeared bleak. Yellow crime scene tape had been wrapped around the perimeter. Large, sloppy black lettering was scribbled across the high-end pane of glass.

"How obnoxious," Lena mumbled as she eyed the damage. "I can only imagine how sick Mr. Young must've felt when he saw this."

"I'm sure he was devastated. And even though the gallery is located in a small town, it is a prominent California exhibition room. Mr. Young has featured premiere artists from all over the world. So to see it being treated like a piece of trash is really disheartening."

"It really is." Lena reached down inside her beige leather hobo bag and grabbed her cell phone. She climbed out of the car and began taking photos of the windows.

"Hey!" she heard someone yell from the doorway. "Is that who I think it is?"

"Mr. Young!" Lena exclaimed, rushing toward the front of the building. "It is so good to see you!"

She embraced the popular curator, surprised by how frail he'd become since the last time she had seen him.

His pale skin was wrinkled with worry. His eyes were sunken in, and the light that once radiated from them had dimmed. The thick blond braid that used to swing down his back had whittled down to a short silver ponytail.

But it wasn't just age that had affected Mr. Young's appearance. Judging by the fearful scowl on his face, he'd clearly been shaken up by the act of vandalism.

"I am so sorry about what happened here," Lena told him. "I hope you don't mind my tagging along with Detective Hudson to analyze the scene."

"Of course not. I don't mind at all. I'm actually glad that an expert such as yourself is here to help."

David approached Mr. Young and shook his hand. "Hello, sir. Lena and I are going to take a look around and try to figure out who did this to your establishment."

"Thank you, Detective. I appreciate that. And hey, you never know. Lena just may end up cracking this case all on her own. She's got that LA expertise under her belt." He reached out and patted her arm. "Speaking of LA, we were all so devastated after hearing that you'd been attacked. I just—the whole town was just…"

"Thanks, Mr. Young," Lena said after his voice broke. "I'm working on putting all that behind me and moving forward. Hopefully being back home with family and friends will help me to do that."

"I'm sure it will," he assured her.

An awkward silence fell over the group. Lena hated how the subject of her attack triggered an uncomfortable energy every time it was brought up. She fiddled with a metal button on her jumpsuit, hoping David would step in and say something.

David cleared his throat and turned to Mr. Young. "So, if it's okay with you, I'd like to take a look at the surveillance tapes. I want to get a good look at the perpetrator and gather whatever evidence can be pulled from the video."

"Of course, Detective. Follow me. I'll take you to the back room where the security system is set up."

Just as the threesome headed inside the gallery, a red pickup truck pulled in front of the building.

Two men jumped out. Lena watched as they pulled buckets and mops from the cargo bed.

"Oh good," Mr. Young said. "My maintenance crew is here. I asked them to come and get rid of this…this *filth*."

"Do you think you could have them hold off on cleaning for now?" Lena asked. "Just until I'm done surveying the scene?"

"Absolutely. Hey, guys?" Mr. Young called out. "Clemmington PD needs to investigate the property before you begin washing down the windows. Would you mind giving them a few minutes? Maybe go next door and grab a coffee while you wait?"

"Sure, no problem, sir," one of the men replied, giving Mr. Young a thumbs-up, then walking over toward Martha's Sip & Savor.

"Okay," Mr. Young continued. "Let's go check out that CCTV footage."

"Listen," Lena said. "Why don't you two go in and start reviewing the footage? I'll stay out here and take a look around before the cleaners come back."

David hesitated, looking up and down the street. "Are you sure? You're okay being out here by yourself?"

Lena tilted her head to the side and emitted a soft chuckle. "Of course I am. And technically, I'm not by myself. I'm standing out on a busy street. Not to mention we're in Clemmington. What's going to happen to me here?"

When David didn't budge, Lena reached out and nudged his shoulder.

"Come on," she teased. "I'm a big girl. Trust me, I'll be fine. I'm just going to search the area for any evidence, then take a few more photos of the graffiti. I'll come inside as soon as I'm done. Okay?"

David craned his neck, staring down the street again as if he was searching for something. Several moments passed before he finally replied.

"Fine. But don't take too long. If you're not inside this gallery in the next fifteen minutes or so, I'm coming back out here."

"Yes, sir," she said, already holding up her cell phone and taking pictures of the window. "See you inside."

Once David was gone, Lena immediately went into investigator mode. She slid her phone inside her back pocket and pulled a pair of latex gloves out of her purse. She slipped them on, then grabbed a plastic baggie and small flashlight.

Lena walked over to the left corner of the building and shined the flashlight down onto the pavement. As she searched the area, a serene feeling floated through her body. Even though she wasn't investigating a high-profile crime scene back in LA, being on a job felt good.

"Come on," she whispered, moving in closer to the building. "Show me something…"

She willed a piece of evidence to appear; a spray-paint bottle or cap that could reveal a fingerprint. Or a piece of clothing accidentally left behind that might match up with the perp's gear in the surveillance footage.

Just as she bent down and studied the gap in between the art gallery and coffee shop next door, a loud car engine roared in the distance.

Lena shot straight up. She peered down the street. A black vehicle slowly turned the corner. She watched as it crept down the road toward the gallery.

Despite memories being triggered by the engine's piercing rumble, Lena turned her attention back to the investigation. But when the noise grew louder, she stood back up and focused on the approaching car.

As Lena got a better look at the vehicle, her limbs went numb. She immediately recognized its obnoxious twenty-four-inch spiked chrome rims. They were attached to the black sports car that chased her from the Cucamonga Wilderness.

"No, no, no, no," Lena whispered. "It can't be him. It *can't* be him!"

The car pulled over toward the curb and stopped abruptly in front of her. She cringed at the sound of its revving engine. A cloud of exhaust billowed from underneath, smoking out the street.

Lena wanted to scream out for David. But she could barely breathe, let alone yell.

Her eyes were glued to the vehicle. She struggled to see inside. But she couldn't make out the person behind the dark tinted windows.

Lena held her breath, waiting for him to jump out and attack.

Don't let him get the best of you this time. Defend yourself. Fight back!

She tried to position her body into a defensive stance. But terror had locked up her arms and legs.

Flashbacks of the assailant slicing his knife into her skin flooded Lena's mind.

I cannot go through that again…

The roar of the engine suddenly ceased. The driver cracked opened the door.

Lena's chest tightened. She recoiled at the sight of a large silver blade.

Just as a black combat boot slipped out of the car and hit the pavement, David came bursting out of the gallery.

"Lena!" he called out while jogging toward her.

She gasped, taking in a huge breath of air. As David approached her, she pointed at the car.

"David! I think that's the—"

But before Lena could finish, the driver slammed the door and sped off.

"Listen," David continued, oblivious to her frightened state, "I've got great news. Miles just texted me. They apprehended the suspect that vandalized the gallery."

Lena stared up at him, blinking rapidly. "Wait..." she uttered, still pointing at what she thought was the suspect's car as it flew around the corner. "They what?"

"They arrested the alleged perp! Officer Underwood was over by the high school and caught some teenager scribbling graffiti across the back of the gymnasium. With black spray paint no less."

"Really?" Lena asked, now wondering if her mind was playing tricks on her. Had she really seen that exact same sports car the night of her attack? Was it an actual knife blade that appeared through the crack of the car door?

Maybe not... Lena thought before turning to David.

"What about the surveillance video?" she asked. "Were you able to get a good look at the perp?"

"I haven't watched it yet. Miles sent the text message letting me know they'd apprehended the suspect right after we sat down. But Mr. Young is going to turn the footage over to me."

"Okay. Good."

Lena felt the tense muscles in her shoulders relax a bit. She knew her attack had left her traumatized. But she didn't realize it'd left her paranoid, as well.

"Let's head back to the station so I can talk to the suspect," David said. "We'll review the surveillance tape once I receive it and see if the young man in the footage resembles the kid they've arrested. Were you able to find any evidence out here?"

"No, I didn't see anything."

Lena contemplated telling David about the man in the black sports car. But she decided against it for fear of sounding neurotic, which would make her appear unstable and land her right back at her parents' house 24/7.

Just stay calm, she told herself. *That man was not your attacker. You're just on edge...*

But as Lena followed David back to the car, she wondered whether she was simply trying to fool herself.

Chapter Six

"A toast," Kennedy said, raising his glass of champagne in the air. "To my oldest son, Jake, formally known as Officer Love, who I am now proud to call *Detective* Love. Congratulations on your promotion, kid."

"Thanks, Dad," Jake said, grinning from ear to ear as he clinked his glass against his father's.

The Love family was standing in the middle of the living room, celebrating Jake's advancement within the department. A few members of the Clemmington PD had joined them, including David.

"Congrats, big bro," Lena said, nudging Jake playfully with her hip.

"Thanks, lil sis. I appreciate it. And hey, I'm glad that you're here to share this moment with me."

David looked on as the two siblings tapped their glasses against one another's, then took a sip of champagne. He smiled, glad to see them healing their rift.

"Yeah, man, congratulations," David chimed in.

"Excuse me, everyone," Betty said. "I hope you didn't get too full of Kennedy's grilled steak, chicken kabobs and corn on the cob, because I'm serving up red velvet cheesecake for dessert."

"Aw, big brother's favorite," Miles teased.

"Shut up, dude," Jake shot back.

Lena leaned into David. "One thing about these two. No matter how old they get, they will never outgrow their sibling rivalry," she whispered.

David chuckled and wrapped his arm around her. "You think this is something? You should see them down at the station. The joke-telling never stops."

"I can only imagine," Lena murmured before looking over at him curiously.

David quickly dropped his arm to his side.

"Oh...sorry," he uttered. "I didn't mean to, um..."

"Relax. It's okay. We didn't just meet yesterday. And I'd like to think that we're friends. Friends can put their arms around one another, can't they?"

"Yeah," he said, his nonchalant shrug a total contradiction of the thrill he felt as her body pressed against his. "Friends should definitely be able to put their arms around one another."

David looked at Lena. Their eyes locked. Just as his gaze drifted down toward her lips, Betty's voice boomed in the background.

"So, if anyone would like a slice of cheesecake, meet me out in the backyard on the deck."

Jake and Miles brushed past Lena so quickly that they almost knocked the glass out of her hand.

"What gentlemen!" she called out, grabbing a napkin and wiping away the champagne that had spilled onto the front of her silk magenta tank dress.

"Sorry!" they yelled in unison.

David picked up a few more napkins off the coffee table and handed them to her. "That won't leave a stain, will it?"

"No, it should be fine once it dries. I just wish my brothers weren't so overzealous over dessert."

Detective Campbell approached the pair. "So maybe that move to LA was good for you after all," he interjected.

Lena paused and turned to him. When she didn't respond, he pressed on.

"You know, because it got you away from your brothers and whatnot."

David watched as Lena's darting eyes filled with apprehension. He could sense that her mind had drifted toward thoughts of the attack.

"I—I don't know, Russ…" she stammered.

"Should we go out onto the deck and grab a slice of cheesecake?" David asked, detecting her discomfort.

"Yes," she responded before the words were barely out of his mouth. "We should."

As David led her outside, Detective Campbell continued to hound her.

"So how's it been, being back in Clemmington?" he queried, probing.

"It's been nice, actually. I've enjoyed reconnecting with my family. And as you know, I've been spending time down at the police station, helping out with some of the investigations."

"Getting back to work so soon hasn't been tough on you after your attack—"

"Hey, Russ," David interrupted, "why don't we lay off of the heavy talk for now. This is a celebration. Let's sip champagne and eat cheesecake and focus on Jake's promotion."

Russ threw his hands in the air as the threesome stepped out onto the deck. "My bad. Sorry, Lena. I was just wondering how you're doing, that's all. I certainly didn't mean to offend you."

"You didn't," she assured him before gently placing her hand on David's arm. "You know how this guy is, though. He's just looking out for me."

"Yeah, well, I wouldn't mind looking out for you, too. Maybe we can get together sometime next week for drinks. Or dinner even. Whatever you're comfortable with."

David clenched his teeth together, resisting the urge to punch Russ in the jaw. The detective was a known ladies' man throughout the town of Clemmington as well as several surrounding areas. Between meeting women online and hanging out at all the hot spots, Russ's contacts list was endless. And he didn't mind bragging about it. The last thing David wanted was for Lena to get caught up with a player like him.

He turned to Lena, anxiously awaiting her response.

"Honestly, Russ," she began, "I'm just focusing on my recovery right now. But I do appreciate the offer. Thank you."

"So I take that as a no, then?"

"Did she stutter?" David shot back, unable to conceal the smirk on his face.

"All right then, Lena," Russ said, slowly backing away while ignoring David. "Maybe some other time."

The cringey exchange was interrupted when Betty walked over and handed David and Lena two slices of cheesecake.

"Here you go," she said. "I wanted to make sure you both got a piece before it's all gone. Kennedy and those sons of mine are already on their second helpings."

"Of course they are," Lena said, then snickered. "Thanks, Mom."

"You're welcome, honey." Betty leaned in and kissed Lena on her cheek. "I know it may not be under the best circumstances, but it certainly is nice having you home. I think I'm getting spoiled."

"Yeah, me, too," David said. When Lena and her mother both turned to him with surprised looks on their faces, he cleared his throat. "I mean, I agree that it's been nice having Lena around. You know, down at the station helping out…"

"Nice save, sweetheart," Betty muttered, patting his arm before walking off.

"Thanks for the cheesecake!" he told her before glancing over at Lena. "That mother of yours is something else."

"Oh, you don't have to tell me. She doesn't miss much. I think it comes from all those years of teaching young, mischievous students."

"I couldn't agree more."

David bit into a mouthful of cheesecake and looked around the Love family's spacious backyard. The lush green lawn was surrounded by colorful philodendron plants and butterfly bushes. The cedarwood fence was lined with bright green horsetail reed bamboo. A Western Redbud tree stood in the middle of the yard, its magenta-colored blossoms blowing gently in the breeze. It was a beautiful setting for the joyous occasion.

"So," he said to Lena, "no interest in Russ, huh."

"Russ *Campbell*? Please. None whatsoever. That man is a known playboy. He's even dated a few of the female LAPD officers. And when they found out about one another? Whew! That drama lasted for a good couple of months around the station."

"Typical Campbell behavior," David said. He took a deep breath, stabbing his fork into his cheesecake before continuing. "So, uh, speaking of dating, are you seeing anyone?"

"Me?" Lena practically choked. "No. Not even close. I've been so wrapped up in my work that I haven't had time to even think about dating." She paused, her eyes squinting as she stared at David. "What about you? Are you seeing anyone?"

"Nah. I'm single as a one-dollar bill."

"Oh, so you're *single* single," she replied before they simultaneously burst out laughing.

"Yep," he replied. "I sure am. Like you, I've been totally focused on work."

"Hmm, interesting..."

David watched as Lena slid a piece of cheesecake into her mouth. He stiffened up at the sight of her glossy lips, puckering as she chewed.

Chill out. You're at your boss's house...

David felt something stirring deep within him. He shifted his feet, anxious to shake it off. He couldn't.

You have got to get out of here...

"Hey, listen," he said. "I, uh, I'd better get going."

"So soon? But what about the fireworks show? You know my dad and Miles are going to surprise Jake with what they're calling *the most epic pyrotechnics display of all time.*"

"Yeah, sorry I'm going to have to miss it. But I, um, I need to get over to my sister's house. I promised her I'd help move some things out of the basement and into the garage."

David didn't feel too bad considering he wasn't lying. Technically. He *had* promised his sister he'd help with the clean out. He just wasn't due to be at her place for another couple of hours.

"Okay." Lena sighed. "Well, thanks for coming by and celebrating with us."

"Of course. Thank you for having me."

"Can I walk you out?"

"No, no," David replied brusquely. "I mean, I'll be fine. You just stay here and enjoy the party."

He hoped she hadn't sensed the abrasiveness in his voice. But David felt an urgent need to leave before he made a fool of himself.

"I guess I'll see you at the station tomorrow, then?" Lena asked.

"Yep, see you tomorrow."

And with that, David charged out of the backyard without saying goodbye to anyone else.

Chapter Seven

Lena gripped the car door handle as David peeled around the corner and flew down Robinson Avenue. He pulled in front of Nancy's Country Mart and slammed on the brakes, double-parking next to a squad car.

The pair jumped out and ran toward the entrance, ducking underneath the yellow crime scene tape on the way inside.

"Was anyone hurt?" David asked Russ, who was standing in the doorway.

"Not that I'm aware of. But double-check with Jake and Miles. They're both inside near the cash register, talking to Nancy."

As the two detectives continued to talk, Lena took a few steps back and eyed the store.

It had been burglarized sometime during the middle of the night. Nancy hadn't discovered the break-in until she arrived to open up earlier that morning.

The mart, which had been a Clemmington staple for years, was one of Lena's favorite stores. Its charming red wooden structure resembled that of an old country barn. Bales of hay were stacked on either side of the white-framed doorway, and miniature pumpkins lined the ramp leading up to the entrance.

The inside of the store looked more like a high-end marketplace. Shiny white oak floors, chrome shelving units and sleek recessed ceiling lights created a sophisticated atmosphere. One side of the mart contained a variety of gourmet meats and cheeses, specialty breads, and international wines. The other side housed unique toys and gifts, luxury beauty products, and a mini floral department.

Today, however, the normally pristine store had been ransacked. The front picture window was shattered. Graffiti had been spray-painted along the walls. A slew of items were strewn across the floor. Silver art display panels had been pulled from the walls, along with the paintings hanging from them.

"Lena, did you remember to bring your forensics kit?" David asked her.

"Of course," she told him, pulling the black plastic case from her tote bag. "I seldom leave home without it."

"Good. Just making sure since we ran out of the station so quickly. I'm gonna head to the back and talk to Nancy and the other officers. Why don't you start processing the scene?"

"I'm on it," Lena replied, pulling a pair of latex gloves out of the pocket of her gray skinny jeans. When David threw her a look, she pulled an extra pair from the pocket of her black leather moto jacket and handed them to him.

"Thanks for looking out for me," he said.

"No worries." She reached inside her forensics kit and grabbed a couple pairs of disposable white shoe coverings. "You'd better put these on, too. Don't want to contaminate the scene."

When he reached for the booties, Lena felt David's fingers glide over her hand. She ignored the shivers that shot up her arm and bent down, slipping the covers over her black combat boots.

"You ready, Hudson?" Russ asked him.

Lena glanced back up and saw that David was still standing there, staring down at her.

"Yeah," he told the detective without taking his eyes off her. "Right behind you."

She slipped past the men. "I'd better get started. David, I'll circle back with you once I survey the store and see what I can find."

"Sounds good. Thanks again for helping us out, Lena. I know you keep hearing this, but we're lucky to have you back home, lending us your expertise."

She turned to him and nodded her head. "Thank you for that. Being back in Clemmington is beginning to feel more and more therapeutic."

"I'm glad to hear it."

The pair stood there, neither breaking their gaze.

Russ cleared his throat and stepped in between them.

"We'd better get moving," he told David.

Judging by the scowl on Russ's face, Lena knew that the suggestion was driven by jealousy rather than business. She backed away, not wanting to take the focus off the investigation.

"I'll catch up with you in a bit," she told David.

Time to get into forensic investigator mode...

Lena slipped on a pair of eye goggles, then pulled a bottle of black granular powder from her kit. She sprinkled the substance along the frames of the broken windows, the kicked-in door and the doorknob. She then used a soft brush to dust off the excess powder. When fingerprints appeared, Lena took photos, then lifted them with clear adhesive tape.

From the corner of her eye, she noticed David talking to a couple of policemen. But his focus was on her. After a few minutes, he walked over.

"How's everything going?" he asked. "You good? Need my help with anything?"

"No, I'm okay. But thank you."

Lena knew that David was worried about her mental state after the attack. She appreciated his concern but wanted to prove that she was fit for the job.

"I was actually able to lift several fingerprints from the store's entryways," she continued while placing the tape on a latent lift card to help preserve the prints. "So we'll run the data through the FBI's Integrated Automated Fingerprint Identification System in hopes of coming up with a match."

"Sounds good." David paused, his soft expression filled with concern. "So, um, are you sure you're—"

"Detective," Lena interrupted. "I thought you were going to speak to Nancy and the other officers about the break-in."

David threw his hands up and took a step back. "I am, I am. I just—I wanted to make sure you feel comfortable being here. This crime scene isn't just graffiti on a window. This one has escalated."

"I'm fine. I promise. Trust me, I've seen much worse. Being here isn't triggering feelings of fear or anxiety. So go on. Do your thing. I'll catch up with you shortly."

"Yes, ma'am."

Once David walked off, Lena turned her attention back to the scene. She walked over to the store's wine display, which had been completely destroyed. Glass bottles were shattered everywhere. The wood crate shelves were crushed. Pools of red and yellow wine covered the floor.

Lena bent down and noticed a stained shard of glass. The deep shade of burgundy didn't appear to be wine. She picked it up and took a closer look.

It was blood.

Excellent, Lena thought, hoping that the evidence would lead them to a suspect.

She pulled a piece of butcher paper out of her bag and carefully wrapped the glass, then slid it inside a brown paper bag and secured it with red evidence tape.

Lena then stood up and continued studying the perimeter. Her eyes landed on a piece of metal sticking out from underneath a rack of T-shirts that had been knocked over.

She stepped carefully through the debris. The rod appeared to be an arm that had broken off the clothing rack. But when Lena grabbed hold of it, she realized that the fixture was actually a steel pipe.

"What have you got there?" she heard Miles call out.

Lena looked up and saw him standing near the floral department, watching her intently. The look of concern in his eyes told her that he too was worried about her well-being.

"I'm thinking it may be a weapon that our perp used to do some of this damage," she told him, her strong tone filled with confidence. It was her way of discreetly letting him know that she was fine. "We'll process it and see what comes up."

Miles gave her a thumbs-up. She nodded her head, then turned her attention back to the scene.

Just as Lena slipped the pipe inside a brown paper bag and sealed it with evidence tape, she heard a loud whimper. Nancy was leaning against the checkout counter, doubled over in tears while her daughter Sarah rubbed her back.

Poor woman, Lena thought. The store owner took so much pride in her establishment.

Lena walked over to the register.

"Nancy, I am so sorry about this burglary."

Her head popped up. Nancy's round, doll-like face was streaked with tears. Her signature brunette beehive, which was normally perfectly coiffed, was completely disheveled.

"Oh, Lena," she wailed, "I'm so glad you're here. Please help me find the *animals* who did this to my beautiful store!"

"I promise you that I will do everything in my power to find them. Have you contacted your insurance company yet?"

"No, not yet," her daughter Sarah replied. "I'm

going to call our agent as soon as I can calm my mom down."

"Okay, good. Once we're done processing the scene, your insurer will send out an adjuster who'll assess the damage. That'll get you on the road to repairing and rebuilding this place. Your beloved market will be back up and running before you know it. I'd also recommend filing a business income and extra expense claim. That way you'll receive a settlement that will cover lost profits while the store is closed for repairs."

"Thank you so much, Lena," Nancy said, wiping her nose with a tissue. "I appreciate that." She backed away from the counter and eyed the store wearily. "Have you found any evidence yet that might identify a suspect?"

"I have, actually. I've got a few items here in these bags that could help us track down the culprit or culprits. I'll know more once we send them off to the crime lab and have them processed."

"Humph. Good luck with that," Russ muttered underneath his breath.

Lena turned around and glanced at the detective, who was standing behind her taking photos of a smashed jewelry display case. He paused, shrugging his shoulders.

"Just being honest," he whispered to her.

Lena subtly shook her head from side to side in hopes of quieting him. They both knew that many of California's crime labs were notoriously backed up. The wait on getting forensic results back could take months. But she didn't want Nancy to hear that, considering how upset she was.

Lena cleared her throat and turned her attention back to the store owner. "I know that you've already been questioned by law enforcement. But I have to ask, do you have any idea who may have done this?"

Nancy stared off into space. Her quivering lips tightened. "No, I don't. Unless it was some punk high school kid. Like the one who vandalized Mr. Young's art gallery. But all he did over there was spray-paint graffiti on the window. Not break in and destroy everything."

When her voice broke, Sarah wrapped her arm around her mother. "It's okay, Mom. We'll rebuild the store. It'll be even better than it was before. And in the meantime, law enforcement will figure out who did this."

"Yes, we will," Lena confirmed.

"I hope so," Nancy sobbed. "I'm just glad we weren't here during the break-in. Can you imagine what would've happened to us if we had been?"

"No," Sarah replied. "But luckily we weren't. So let's not even think about that." She tightened her grip on her mother's shoulder before turning to Lena. "Do you know if anyone has checked around the outside of the store yet?"

"Detective Hudson and a few other officers are examining the front now."

"What about the back? Have you seen it?"

"No, not yet."

Nancy's eyes filled with a fresh batch of tears. "Please, go look. Paint's been splattered all over the back exterior. My sunset mural is completely ruined!"

"And there's a strange message spray-painted across the top of it," Sarah added.

"Really?" Lena asked. "What does it say?"

Sarah tapped her fingernails against the counter and stared up at the ceiling. "You know, I don't remember. But it reads like some kind of weird nursery rhyme. You'll see it when you go out there."

"Okay. I'll go check it out now."

"Thank you," Nancy mumbled before leaning over and propping her head against her daughter's arm.

Seeing the store owner so distraught caused a hot streak of anger to shoot straight through Lena. She set her evidence bags down behind the counter, then marched toward the back of the store, bursting through the exit.

She stepped out into the alleyway. Aside from a few nearby dumpsters, the vicinity was empty.

Lena stared up at the store's red wooden wall. Obnoxious splatters of paint covered the mural's green palm trees and orange setting sun. Graffitied words were scrawled above it.

She moved farther into the alley, shielding her eyes from the sun while studying the phrase.

Three Four Kicking Down Your Door, it read.

"Yeah, you kicked down the door all right," Lena muttered. "And did a whole lot worse."

She pulled out her camera. As she began taking photos of the wall, Lena paused.

"'Three four kicking down your door,'" she said out loud.

Her mind flashed back to the message left on Mr. Young's gallery window.

One Two I Am Coming For You...

Just as Lena began to make the connection, she heard the roar of a thunderous car engine.

Lena froze. A burst of panic imploded inside her chest. She dropped her camera down by her side and stumbled toward the doorway.

Her head swiveled from right to left. She peered down each end of the alleyway. There were no cars in sight.

It's nothing, she told herself. *Maybe it's just—*

Before she could finish convincing herself, the engine roared once again.

"Okay," she whispered. "This is happening. This is really happening. *Again.*"

Lena tried to spin around and run back inside the store. But just like a nightmare, her body suddenly became immobilized. That numbing fear returned, seeping through her limbs like venomous snake poison.

Get back inside the store. Get back inside the store!

The words reverberated through her mind. But her legs refused to cooperate. The only thing she could move was her head.

Once again, there was no sign of a car. Yet there was the sound of approaching footsteps.

Oh good. Law enforcement is finally making their way back here...

Lena leaned her stiff body against the wall. She inhaled slowly as the footsteps drew nearer.

But then she realized that they weren't coming from inside the store. They were coming down the alleyway.

Heart palpitations thumped against Lena's rib cage. The sound of the pounding shoe soles reminded her of the moment she was being chased down the Cucamonga Wilderness hiking trail. She closed her eyes and held her breath, desperate for someone to show up and rescue her.

The footsteps quickened. Lena forced her eyes open. She scanned the alley.

A man dressed in green camo army fatigues was charging toward her. His face was covered in a full mask. Tactical gloves and military boots covered his hands and feet.

Lena winced as his eyes penetrated hers. He balled his hands into tight fists, swinging his arms in rhythm with his legs. When he seemed to notice her watching him, his speed increased.

This is it. I am going to die. With all of Clemmington's law enforcement officers right inside this store, I'm gonna die.

Just when the man stopped a few feet away from Lena, David came flying through the back door.

"Hey!" he said. "Guess what?"

Lena was unable to speak. She could only lean over and crumble into David's arms.

"What's going on?" he asked her just as the man in the fatigues approached them.

"Hey, what's up, Lena?" the man said.

Her head swiveled. She looked over at him. He removed the mask, revealing a handsome bearded face that was smiling from ear to ear.

"Ryan!" Lena practically screamed before swatting his chest. "You just scared me half to death! Why were you charging at me like that?"

"Sorry. I was in the middle of a run when I heard that my mom's store had been burglarized. So I got down here as fast as I could."

"And what's up with the outfit?" David asked him. "Getting ready for basic training early?"

"Yes, sir. I'm due to arrive at Fort Benning in Columbus, Georgia, next month. When I get there, I want to be as prepared as possible."

"Fort Benning, huh," David replied. "So you're going out for the infantry. That's gonna be pretty tough, you know."

"I do know. Both physically and psychologically. But I'll be ready."

"I bet you will. Why don't you go around to the front of the store and have your mom step outside? I've still got my team inside processing the crime scene. I don't want anything to contaminate the potential evidence."

"Will do, Detective Hudson. Do you all have any idea who may have done this?"

"Not yet," Lena told him after finally pulling herself together. "But we're working on it."

"Good. I hope you catch the bastard soon."

"That's our hope," David assured him.

Once Ryan headed to the front of the store, Lena turned to David. She contemplated telling him how terrified she'd been while watching Ryan charge down the alleyway.

Nope, she told herself. *Keep your mouth shut. He already questioned whether or not you were mentally ready to be here in the first place...*

"I've got good news," David said.

"I could use some good news right now. What's up?"

"Nancy pulled me to the side after overhearing Russ discussing how long the crime lab may take to process the evidence."

"Oh no," Lena moaned. "I tried to shut him up about that. Nancy's already so distraught. I didn't want him adding to that."

"Well, her anger prompted me to call down to the lab and ask if we could bring the evidence there and process it ourselves."

Lena reached out and gripped David's arm. "*Really?* And? What'd they say?"

"They said yes."

"David, that is awesome! I can't believe they're giving us personal access to the lab."

"Trust me, the facility director was very hesitant until I told her that the famed, highly skilled Lena Love would be the one processing the evidence. I couldn't get your name out of my mouth before she told me that we're more than welcome to utilize the lab."

"Aw, how nice of her. I'm flattered. By her *and* you. So, thank you."

"Just stating the facts. She did say we'd better get down there soon because they're extremely busy. Were you able to find any viable evidence other than the fingerprints?"

"I was. I'll show you everything once we get to the lab."

As the pair headed back inside the store, David paused, staring up at the vandalized mural.

"Wow," he breathed. "Whoever broke into this place was out for blood. What a vicious attack."

"Did you see the graffiti they scribbled at the top?"

David took a step back. "'Three four kicking down your door,'" he read. He crossed his arms in front of him, his eyes blinking rapidly. "That phrase is a continuation of the message that was spray-painted on Mr. Young's window. Remember? 'One two I am coming for you'?"

"I do remember. I was actually putting that together just as Ryan came charging toward me. What do you think it means? That our perp has a personal vendetta against Mr. Young *and* Nancy?"

David didn't immediately respond. His jaws clenched, as if he were holding something in.

"I don't know," he finally said. "But we'll figure it out. In the meantime, let's get back inside the store and finish processing the scene so that we can head to the lab."

"Right behind you."

Chapter Eight

"You know," Lena said, "I have to admit, I was pretty disappointed after I failed to collect any evidence from Mr. Young's art gallery."

"Well, now's your big chance to help us figure out who broke into Nancy's store," David told her. "So have at it."

She and David were standing at a corner station inside the Definitive Solutions Crime Lab. Lena was busy processing the evidence while he looked on.

She slipped on a pair of latex gloves, opened one of the brown paper bags and pulled out the metal pipe.

David leaned in and inspected it. "My guess is that our suspect used the pipe to shatter the windows and damage items inside the store."

"I think you're right."

Lena placed the pipe inside a cyanoacrylate fuming chamber and closed its clear glass door.

"Now, what is this thing?" David asked, pointing at the large square machine. "It looks like an oversize kitchen cabinet."

"This machine develops latent fingerprints on evidentiary objects. Hopefully it'll capture any prints that were left on the pipe."

"And how do you make that happen?"

"Well, I'm going to start by adding cyanoacrylate, which is a strong, fast-acting adhesive, to the chamber's heating element. Then I'll set the fuming cycle time. After that, I'll hit the start button and begin the process."

David peered inside the machine. "And what happens once it starts...*fuming*?"

"Right. Fuming." Lena glanced over at David, enticed by the inquisitive expression on his handsome face.

Focus, she told herself before turning back to the machine.

"Once the fuming process begins, vapors from the adhesive will blend with the machine's humidity. Those fumes stick to the fingerprint residue on the pipe, which will reveal the print's ridges. Once that's done, the pipe will be ready for forensic analysis. If the fingerprints match someone's in your system, then, voilà. We'll be able to identify our suspect."

"That is absolutely fascinating," David said, his wide eyes revealing his awe.

When he gave her a round of applause, she curtsied. "Thank you very much."

Once Lena got the fuming process going, she took a deep breath and glanced around the bustling laboratory.

The stark white floors and walls were spotless. Staffers dressed in lab coats and protective eye goggles shuffled past long steel tables. The workstations were packed with techs injecting chemicals into test tubes, studying samples through microscopes and importing information into computer software systems.

"Hey," Lena said, "any word on whether Nancy turned over the store's surveillance footage yet?"

"I don't know. Let me check." David pulled out his cell phone and tapped the notifications. "Oh, Miles just texted me a few minutes ago. They've got the footage. They're reviewing it now."

"Good." Lena picked up another brown paper bag and opened it. "I just wish there were eyewitnesses who would've come forward with some sort of information."

"There may be. You never know. We posted news of the break-in on Clemmington PD's website as well as our social media accounts, and included the tip hotline. So we could still receive information anonymously. Especially now that Nancy has put up a reward."

"That's true. Rewards do oftentimes attract credible tips."

Lena changed gloves and pulled out the shard of glass. David stared down at the fragment.

"Wow," he breathed. "Judging by the amount of blood on that thing, our suspect must have a really nasty cut somewhere on his or her body."

"I'd say so. And once they're identified, that wound could link them to the crime scene."

Lena placed the piece of glass on a clean board, then picked up a handheld X-ray fluorescence spectrometer.

"Okay, now what is that thing?" David asked. "It looks like a grocery store scanner."

"Okay, so we've gone from a kitchen cabinet to a grocery store scanner, huh," Lena said. "This is actually an XRF analyzer. It's a device used to test the chemical composition of materials. So in other words, it collects potential biological evidence."

"Gotcha. You know, I've never actually watched any of these forensic testing procedures. It's pretty amazing. You have no idea how impressed I am with you right now."

"Why thank you. But I'm just doing my job."

"Quite well, might I add…"

Lena glanced over at David. His crooked grin was filled with flirtation. She cleared her throat and quickly turned her attention back to the analysis.

"You know," she said, "we had to drive forty miles outside Clemmington to get to this lab. The facility services several counties. *And* they're short-staffed. The wait time on processing evidence is ridiculous. You should talk to my father about ordering a few pieces of forensic equipment and setting up a small lab inside Clemmington's police station."

David dropped his head as he side-eyed Lena. "And who's gonna pay for all that?"

"I'm sure there's enough money in the town's budget to cover it. Plus my dad is good friends with the mayor. I imagine he'd make an exception for something so important."

David waved his arm around the lab. "Lena, Clemmington could never afford all of this—"

"David," she interrupted, "you don't need all this. Just the basics. A fuming chamber similar to the one I'm using, a tamper resistant drying cabinet to safely store evidence, a high power microscope, extraction software for digital evidence and the XRF analyzer."

He sighed dramatically and leaned against the table. "Okay, so say we do get the green light to install a lab. Who's gonna run it? No one on our staff knows how to operate all that fancy equipment."

Lena turned away from David and stared inside the chamber. Her skin tingled under his intense gaze as he awaited her response.

"You'll just have to hire a forensic scientist," she told him. "I'm sure there's someone out there who would love to work for the Clemmington PD."

"*Someone?* What about you? I mean, you do seem pretty happy being back here. And let's not forget, your father does run the police department. I think it'd be cool for you to work with him and your brothers, especially now that you all seem to have healed that rift. Not to mention…"

David hesitated. Lena watched as he broke eye contact, focusing on the shard of glass lying on the table rather than her.

"Not to mention what?" she asked.

"I—well, I hope I'm not speaking out of turn here. But I just think that you're over LA. Especially after the…"

"The attack?" she queried after his voice trailed off.

Her chest tightened at the sound of those words. She inhaled deeply, struggling to ease the pressure.

Breathe. Calm down... she told herself.

"Yes," David murmured. "After the attack. All I'm saying is that you may feel more comfortable being back here in Clemmington."

"Is there any other reason why you think I should move back?"

"Well, I mean, I'm here, too—"

The loud buzzing of the fuming chamber's timer cut David off.

Lena jumped, startled by the noise. She was also disappointed that it had interrupted the moment.

She waited to see if David would finish his statement. He didn't.

Lena glanced down at her watch. "We'd better get the rest of this evidence processed before the lab director kicks us out. The facility will be closing soon."

"With the famous Lena Love working inside it? I highly doubt that. I'm sure the director will make an exception and stay open late for us."

"Let's not push it. Plus I'm starving. I haven't eaten all day."

"Neither have I," David said. "Why don't we go to The Dearborn Grill for dinner after we're done here? Misty is serving up her spicy glazed salmon tonight."

"Mmm, that sounds delicious. I'd love to."

"Cool. I'll step out and make a reservation while you finish up. Be right back."

Lena watched as he jogged toward the exit. Just as she became fixated on his flexing biceps, the fuming chamber's buzzer went off once again.

Stay focused, she told herself. *You're here to recuperate, not reignite an old flame...*

"THANKS TO YOU," Lena said, "I am now dying to try that spicy glazed salmon. But I'm gonna need a nice glass of Riesling to go along with it."

"I second that," David said. He steered the car around a corner and headed toward the restaurant. "And I'm off the clock, too. So you can't report me to your father and tell him I was drinking on the job."

"Ha ha, very funny."

Lena's cell phone buzzed. She pulled it from her handbag and opened it using the face ID feature. An email message from an unfamiliar address popped up on the screen.

Unknown@Unknown.com

The subject read, *Five Six Up To My Old Tricks...*

Lena's phone almost fell from her hand. She stared straight ahead, focusing on nothing in particular as a sickening chill seeped through her pores.

She thought about Mr. Young's vandalized window.

One Two I Am Coming For You...

And Nancy's mural.

Three Four Kicking Down Your Door...

Her breath caught in her throat.

These attacks have been aimed at me, she thought before sliding down in her seat.

She peered back down at the phone. The body of the email was blank. But there was an attachment.

Lena's index finger trembled as she double-clicked on it. She held her breath while waiting for the attachment to load.

A sketch of a bloody, half-shaped heart appeared on the screen. It matched the scar that her attacker had carved into her chest.

She slowly turned to David.

"He's coming after me," she whispered.

"What?"

"He's coming after me," she repeated, a little louder this time. *"Again."*

"Who's coming after you again?"

"The serial killer."

David stopped at a red light and looked over at her. "Why would you say that?"

"He just emailed this to me."

She held up her phone and showed him the sketch. David leaned toward her, squinting his eyes as he studied the image.

"What is that?" he asked.

Lena forgot that David didn't know about the killer's knife attack on her. She took a deep breath, wiping away tears while summoning the courage to tell that part of the story.

"You know how the killer leaves his signature mark on his victims by carving a heart into their chests with a blade?" she asked.

"I do."

"Well, when I was attacked, the killer began carving a heart into mine. But I was able to get away before he could finish. So he left me with a scar in the form of a half-shaped heart."

"Oh, Lena," David whispered.

When the light turned green, he hit the accelerator, then reached over and clutched her hand. "I am so sorry. I had no idea the assault was that vicious."

She reached up and pressed her other hand against her chest. "No one knew. I asked the LAPD to keep that information confidential. I wasn't ready to talk about it. That part…that was just too much."

"I completely understand."

"And the subject of the email says, 'Five six up to my old tricks.' The killer is the one who vandalized the art gallery, and Nancy's store."

Lena felt as though her chest was caving in. She tried to take a breath as panic sucked the air out of her lungs.

"That's what it's looking like," David agreed quietly. "That high school kid we suspected of vandalizing Mr. Young's store never admitted to it. He only confessed to spray-painting the school's gymnasium. And since we couldn't get a clear visual of the suspect in the gallery's surveillance video, we couldn't charge him for both crimes."

Lena locked her phone, unable to look at the bloody half-shaped heart any longer.

"I think those two vandalisms happening on the same day was a complete coincidence," she said. "It's clear that the killer is doing all of this to alert me that he's here in Clemmington and coming after me. We've got to figure out a plan of action."

David's temples pulsated as he ground his teeth in frustration. "For starters, you're going to have to keep a low profile around town from here on out. Be careful with the apps you use on your cell phone so that he can't track your location. You never know what type of software that maniac has in his possession. And if you post on social media, make sure your location tracker is turned off."

"I will," Lena said, opening the settings app on her phone and confirming that the GPS locator was turned off. "What else?"

"Forward that email to me. I'll have our digital forensic investigator take a look at it and see if he can trace the sender's IP address back to a specific individual. And as a precaution, we're going to have eyes on you twenty-four seven. Do you feel safe staying at your parents' house? If not, you're more than welcome to stay with me."

Lena was surprised by his offer. Before she could respond, David continued. "Wait, I hope that wasn't too forward. I mean, it's not like you don't have your dad there with you, and two law enforcement brothers stopping by regularly. I just—I figure that I should at least offer."

"And I appreciate it. But I should be fine at my parents' place. However, whenever my father's not home and my brothers aren't around, it would be nice if I could have a squad car out front watching over the house."

"Of course. We can definitely make that happen.

And it goes without saying that I'll be keeping an eye on you, as well."

"I'd appreciate that, David."

He slowed down as they approached the restaurant. "Are you sure you're still up for dinner?"

"Definitely. After this new development, I'm really in need of that glass of wine. Or two."

"Same here," he agreed.

David pulled into the parking lot and maneuvered the car into a space near the entrance. He then turned to Lena, reaching out and once again clutching her hand.

"Listen. I want you to know that I've got your back. And I promise not to let anything happen to you again."

"Thank you," she whispered.

Despite the terror surrounding the situation, Lena was overcome by a comforting sense of security. And in that moment, she knew there was no one else she'd rather have protecting her than David.

Chapter Nine

David rocked back in his chair. He propped his hands on top of his head and stared up at the ceiling.

"I cannot believe this is happening," he muttered. "What a nightmare."

Miles, who was sitting on the other side of David's desk, nodded his head in agreement. "Yeah, we've gotta figure something out here. I cannot see my sister go through another attack. Or worse…"

There was a knock at the door.

"Come in!" David called out.

Jake opened the door and shuffled inside. "Sorry I'm late, guys. I was in the chief's office, giving him a rundown on what's going on with Lena."

"How's he doing?" David asked. "Is he all right?"

"He's hanging in there. You know he's a tough guy. But underneath it all he's worried. And pissed off. And ready to hunt down this psychopath who's coming after his baby girl."

"You did tell him not to share the news with Mom yet, didn't you?" Miles asked.

"Of course. He said he'll hold off for now. But eventually, she needs to know."

"Well, I'm planning on making sure we've got eyes on the house twenty-four seven," David said.

"And my dad has law enforcement patrolling the streets," Jake added. "They're on the lookout for anyone or anything that appears suspicious."

"Good." David sat up straight in his chair and pointed over at Miles. "Did you stop by your parents' house on the way to the station this morning?"

"I did. I checked in on Lena. And I dropped off coffee and muffins from her favorite bakery to try and lift her spirits."

"How's she doing?"

"She appears to be hanging in there." Miles sighed. "But you know how she is. She'll never let us see her sweat."

"True," Jake said. "But underneath that tough exterior, I'm sure she's terrified."

"Yeah, well, she wasn't afraid to express her disdain in having to sit around the house all day," Miles said. "Believe it or not, she wanted to come down to the station and check up on the evidence that was collected at Nancy's."

David shook his head. "That woman. I'll give her a call and let her know that Russ is taking over the forensic aspect of the investigation—"

David was interrupted by another knock at the door. "Come in!"

He looked up, shocked to see Lena burst inside his office.

"Lena!" he exclaimed. "What are you doing here? How did you even get here? I thought I told you not to leave the house without letting me know in advance—"

"Look, we can talk about that later," she interrupted, marching right past Jake and Miles. She approached the side of David's desk and slid her tablet computer in front of him. "Take a look at this."

David leaned down and focused on the bright screen. It was set to the front page of the *Los Angeles Times*.

"What am I looking at here?" he asked her.

"Check out the main headline at the top of the page."

David pressed his fingertips against the screen and enlarged the page. "'LA's heart-carving serial killer strikes again,'" he read aloud. "'Another murder victim found.'"

"Wait, when did this happen?" Miles asked.

"According to the article, yesterday," Lena told him. "The same day that Nancy's Country Mart was burglarized."

"So what do you think?" Jake asked. "Is the killer going back and forth between LA and Clemmington to commit these crimes?"

"Or do we have a copycat killer on our hands?" Miles questioned.

Lena groaned loudly, throwing her arms out at her sides. "Who knows? Either of you could be right."

"This is truly baffling," David said while scrolling through the article. "The thing that worries me is that we seem to be dealing with a spree killer. The man is murdering his victims pretty closely together, without taking much of a cooling-off period in between attacks."

"What are the details of this latest killing?" Jake asked.

"It says here that the victim's body was found by hikers, deep inside the Angeles National Forest's Cooper Canyon. They haven't revealed the identity because some of the family members have yet to be notified. But she was in her early thirties, petite and brunette. She was found strangled with her hands tied behind her back. And a wound had been sliced into her chest in the shape of a heart."

David glanced up at Lena. His eyes inadvertently traveled down to her chest. He quickly looked away, hoping he hadn't made it obvious that he was thinking of her scar.

"Yep, that's the killer's modus operandi," Lena said, not seeming to notice. "He's followed that same ritual with each of his victims. And who knows. It could be that the killer isn't working alone."

"Which would make this case that much more complicated," David told her. "Have you spoken to LAPD's chief about this?"

"No, not yet. As soon as the article alert pinged on my phone, I skimmed it and drove straight here."

"Which you should not have done," Jake retorted. "Like David said, we want eyes on you at all times. Until we catch this killer, we don't want you roaming around town alone."

"Yeah, well, I figured if the killer is busy committing crimes in LA, he can't be in Clemmington right now—"

"Lena," David interrupted, "we don't know what this psycho is up to. So we need to take all the precautions that we can. As the saying goes, better safe than sorry."

"I know, I know. So what's our new course of action?"

David handed her the tablet. "Why don't you start by calling LAPD's chief? Find out if they have any updates on the case. Was there any evidence at the scene? Are they any closer to catching the killer? While we're busy trying to come up with a course of action, I'd like to know theirs. And—"

David was interrupted by a knock on his door frame.

The foursome turned around. Chief Love was standing in the doorway, a stern expression on his face.

"Lena, what are you doing here?" he asked. "You're supposed to be at home, laying low."

She stormed over to her father and handed him the tablet. "This is why I'm here."

Chief Love scanned the article. The further in he read, the deeper his eyebrows furrowed.

"Humph, another murder," he said, sighing. The chief scrolled down to the end of the article. "But wait, if he committed this murder in LA yesterday, are we sure he's the one who burglarized Nancy's store?"

"That's what we're trying to figure out," Lena told him.

"Well, keep me posted. I'm glad to know I've got four great minds inside this office working on the case."

"Five, counting yours," Jake chimed in.

"Thanks, son." Chief Love paused, wrapping his arm around Lena. "I'm hopeful that together with the LAPD, we'll catch this psycho soon. In the meantime, I need to get back to my office and return Nancy's five phone calls. According to Milly, she's anxious to find out whether we've identified a suspect. Speaking of which," he continued, turning to David, "what's the latest on those forensic lab results?"

David grabbed his notebook and flipped it open. "I spoke with the lab director this morning. She's put a rush order on the results. So it's just a matter of time before I get them back. And Russ is running the fingerprints that Lena lifted through the FBI's ID system."

"Let me know as soon as you've got something. And as for you," Chief Love said, giving Lena's shoulder a gentle squeeze, "let this be the last time you leave the house alone. Especially without telling one of us first. We can't afford to take any chances at this point."

"Yes, sir," she mumbled.

David watched as Lena picked imaginary lint off her emerald green tunic. He felt for her, knowing how anxious she was to help with the investigation but having to stand down because she was a target.

"All right, then," the chief said. "I'll let you four get back to it while I call Nancy."

As soon as he left the office, Lena grabbed a chair from the corner and pulled it up to the desk. She sat down, then removed her notebook and a pen from her handbag.

David looked over at Jake and Miles. The three of

them stared at one another, their expressions weary. It was clear that they were all worried about her.

David cleared his throat. "So, uh, Lena? How are you feeling after finding out that the killer has struck again? Are you okay?"

She snapped the top off her pen and began scribbling in her notebook.

"Yes," she replied without looking up. "I'm fine. Just ready to get to work and start planning our course of action. So, what are we thinking? Where do we go from here?"

The determination behind her stoic expression was chilling. David was in awe of her fearlessness.

"Well, for starters," he began, "I'm thinking we should probably order lunch. Looks like it's gonna be a long day inside the station."

"I agree," Miles said. "We've got a lot to unpack here."

Jake stood up and walked over to the whiteboard. He grabbed a black marker and wrote the words *Next Steps: BOLO*.

"Okay," he said. "While you all think about what you want to order, let's talk about the suspect. What do we know about him? How does he look? What does he usually wear? What kind of car may he be driving?"

All eyes turned to Lena since she was the killer's only surviving victim.

"Well," she said, shifting in her seat, "I didn't get a good look at his face because he was wearing a mask. But I do know that he's got cold, pale gray eyes. He looked to be about five feet eleven inches or so. Slightly stocky build. And he was dressed in tactical camouflage gear."

David could see a change in Lena's disposition. Seeing her in distress caused his chest muscles to tighten.

"And he drives a black sports car with a really loud engine and huge, spiked chrome wheels."

"How do you know what kind of car he drives?" David asked.

"I, um… I saw a car here in Clemmington that looked similar to a vehicle that chased after me the night I was attacked."

"What?" both Jake and Miles yelled in unison. David was too stunned to even speak. He held his hand up in an attempt to calm her brothers, who were now gathering around her.

"Lena," David said in a calm voice, "why didn't you report that to us? Don't you think it's something we should've been made aware of, so that we could—"

"No!" she insisted, jumping up from her chair and pacing the floor. Jake and Miles immediately backed off. "I shouldn't have made you all aware of it. You know why? Because everybody would've thought I was being paranoid. And suffering from PTSD. And you would've forced me to sit inside the house nonstop even sooner than you already have."

Her voice broke. David stood up and walked around the desk. When he put his arm around her, she quieted down and leaned her head against his chest.

"Guys," he said to Jake and Miles, "could you please give us a minute?"

They both nodded their heads. Miles gently

squeezed Lena's arm on the way out the door. "Sorry if it seems like we're ganging up on you—"

"*Seems,*" she interrupted sarcastically.

"You know what I mean. We're just worried about you."

When Lena remained silent, David spoke up.

"Thanks, Miles. Hey, would you mind asking Milly to order us a couple of pizzas and cartons of iced tea from Ronaldo's?" He quickly looked down at Lena. "Wait, are you good with pizza?"

"I don't have much of an appetite. But sure. Get whatever you all want."

"Will do," Miles said before following Jake out of the office.

Once the door was closed, David led Lena over to a chair.

"Why don't you have a seat. Let's talk."

She sat down slowly, staring down at her hands.

"David?" she whispered. "If you all don't allow me to stay involved in this investigation, I'm afraid the killer will never be caught."

David paused. He sat down next to her and held her hand.

"I can understand why you feel that way. You're highly skilled at what you do. But we've got to keep you safe, Lena. Which means you can't keep anything from us. If you see something, you have to say something. Don't let your passion for your work get you killed. Deal?"

"Deal."

"And with that being said, I really think you should

consider stepping away from the investigation. Take a break. Let the police handle the—"

"No," Lena interrupted. "I will not back down from this case, David."

He fell silent for several moments before responding.

"Understood."

David instinctively leaned down and kissed her softly on the forehead. She raised her head. Their lips were inches apart. Just as the pair moved in closer, there was a knock at the door.

They both jumped back.

"Come in!" David called out, much louder than necessary.

Jake and Miles shuffled inside the office.

"Your boss sent us back in here," Jake told them. "He said that if we don't get to work immediately and start putting a plan in place, he's gonna fire us all."

"That man…" Lena said, slowly shaking her head.

David quickly walked back around his desk and took a seat, hoping the brothers hadn't noticed him and Lena getting close to one another.

"All right then," he said. "Let's get to it."

Chapter Ten

Lena rolled over onto her back and stared up at the clouds painted across her bedroom ceiling. She pressed her fingertips into her temples and rubbed them rigorously. Being cooped up in her parents' house had left her head spinning.

Or maybe it's the fact that you keep your eyes glued to that tablet...

Even though Lena suspected she may have been suffering from a bout of cybersickness, she grabbed her iPad and pull up the *Los Angeles Times'* website.

Do not read that article again. Do not read that article again...

But Lena ignored the voice in her head and began scanning the latest report on the serial killer for the hundredth time.

It is believed that the unidentified victim is their killer's seventh attack, the article read. The sixth was Lena Love, LAPD's own forensic investigator. She was assaulted while processing the fifth victim's crime scene on the Cucamonga Wilderness hiking trail. Unlike the killer's other victims, Love survived the attack.

According to Herschel Scott, LAPD's chief of police, Love was on the cusp of catching their elusive killer.

"Trust me, Lena was on his heels, and he knew it," Chief Scott told reporters. "I believe that's what drove his attack. Had Lena not been assaulted, the killer would be in police custody right now."

Love has since taken a leave of absence from the force. We here at the *Los Angeles Times* wish her a speedy recovery.

Lena slammed the tablet down onto the bed. She tossed off her frilly white comforter and jumped up, frantically pacing the floor.

"I should not be stuck in this house," she said to herself. "I should be on the scene, helping to catch the killer!"

"Lena?" her mother called out. "Are you talking to me?"

"No! I—I was leaving someone a voice mail," she lied, so that her mother wouldn't think she was losing her mind.

Even though it feels like I am.

"All right," her mother said. "I made coffee if you want a cup. And Miles dropped off your favorite muffins again this morning on the way to work. They're in the kitchen."

"Thanks! I'll be out in a minute."

Lena skulked over to the window. She parted the embroidered cream curtains and glanced up and down the bustling street. Neighbors were out and about, tending to the lawns surrounding their bungalows and ranch-style homes, jogging along the winding road's sidewalk and carrying groceries into their homes.

She stared up at the swaying palm trees. The sight made her long to be back in LA, working on the case that had grown so personal.

If only you could turn back the hands of time, she thought, wishing she hadn't gone out to that hiking trail alone.

Right before Lena stepped away from the window, she noticed the ever-present squad car parked a couple of houses down. It was a constant reminder that she was being hunted by a crazed maniac.

"Ugh," she moaned. "Time to go out and relive the same day over again."

Lena took a quick shower, then slipped into a lavender sweatshirt, black leggings and a pair of sneakers.

She left her bedroom and headed to the kitchen. On the way there, she heard her mother whispering hysterically.

"Where was the body found?" Betty hissed. "On the *Juniper hiking trail*? Oh no, Kennedy. Lucinda and I used to walk that trail all the time. That is terrifying! What do you think happened to her?"

Lena hovered closer to the kitchen door. Her mother was leaning against the sink, gripping the phone to her ear.

"I cannot believe something like this has happened

here. In *Clemmington*. And you said the victim was strangled?"

"Oh my God," Lena whispered into her palm.

"Well, if there was a heart carved into her chest," Betty uttered, "that means it must be the same killer who attacked our—"

Her voice broke as she emitted a long sob. "I'm sorry. I'm trying to be strong, Kennedy. But I just… I hope this isn't a warning that he's coming after our daughter next!"

Lena fell against the wall. The nerves in her legs weakened underneath the weight of her mother's words. A bout of nausea hit her stomach. She tried to swallow the lump of panic climbing up her throat. But her mouth was so dry that she almost choked instead.

"I know," Betty continued. "I promise that I'll hold it together for the sake of Lena…No, of course not. I won't mention a thing. I'll act as if nothing has happened. You just better make sure this doesn't leak to the press…All right. Call me as soon as you've got an update. Be careful…I love you, too."

Lena quickly stepped away from the kitchen doorway just as her mother disconnected the call. She walked over to the living room's Victorian bay windows, running her sweaty hands down her leggings while staring outside.

"Lena?"

"Yes!" she practically screamed after being startled by her mother's loud tone.

"Are you coming for your coffee and muffin?"

Lena hurried through the living room and entered

the kitchen. When she noticed the lingering tears still glistening in her mother's eyes, her gaze fell to the beige stone tiles.

"Yep," she said, struggling to sound upbeat despite what she'd just heard.

Betty spun around and busied herself at the counter. "I'll get you a cup and saucer."

Lena wanted to rush up to her mother and hug her. But she didn't want to appear as though she'd overheard the conversation. So instead, she walked over to the sliding glass doors and looked out into the backyard.

Her Jeep, which was parked in front of the garage door, came into view. And then, she was overcome by that all too familiar urge.

Lena's arms fell down by her sides. She balled her hands into tight fists, then released them, then balled them up again. Her feet shuffled from right to left, as if she were at the starting line of a race and preparing to take off. Her mind began to shift. Everything around her shut down. Nothing else mattered, except getting to that crime scene.

"Lena, are you okay?" Betty asked.

She swiveled around. Her mother was standing at the breakfast nook placing a cup of coffee and platter of muffins on the table. Her eyes appeared as though they'd finally stopped weeping. But her lips were now twisted with concern.

"Yeah, Mom. I'm fine."

Lena glanced down at the nook's padded blue bench. Her purse was sitting on the edge.

"You know what?" she continued. "I think I'm gonna have my coffee and muffin out on the deck. Get some sun, meditate, maybe even do some yoga."

"I think that would be good for you, sweetheart."

Betty walked over and wrapped her arms around Lena, squeezing tightly. Then she planted a series of kisses all over her face, just like she used to do when Lena was a child.

"Mom!" Lena squealed. "That tickles!"

"I know. And I don't care. You're never too old to be showered with love and affection by your mama."

"Yes, ma'am," Lena said, giving her a firm hug.

"Okay." Betty sighed. She stepped away from her daughter while dabbing her eyes. "I'd better go take these rollers out of my hair and put on a little makeup. I've got a video conference call with a couple of my mentees from the women's group. They're new to teaching this year, and I promised I'd help them enhance their curriculums."

"Aw, that's sweet. Well, while you're doing that, I'll be out on the deck."

"Sounds good. Enjoy yourself, baby."

Lena watched as Betty walked out of the kitchen. Once she was gone, Lena tiptoed toward the entryway, sticking her ear toward the living room. As soon as she heard her mother's bathroom door close, Lena darted back into the kitchen and snatched her purse.

She slipped out of the sliding glass door. After glancing around to make sure that the coast was clear, she jumped inside her car and sped off toward the Juniper hiking trail.

LENA SLOWLY DROVE past the street where the hiking trail's entrance was located. The block had been cordoned off with yellow tape. The entire road was swarming with squad cars, their red-and-blue lights flashing.

Several law enforcement officers were pacing the road. They waved their arms at a few of the residents who lived on the upscale block, motioning for them to go back inside their homes.

"How in the hell are you going to get to this crime scene?" Lena asked herself.

She was very familiar with the trail. She and her friends had hiked it for years. There were several ways of accessing the area that didn't involve entering through the designated entrance.

Lena pulled her phone out of her purse and checked the home screen. There were no new notifications. She was surprised that David hadn't reached out to tell her what was going on. While she was slightly irritated, Lena knew that he was only looking out for her mental well-being.

She contemplated calling and telling him that she was there, then asking if he'd let her through to help examine the crime scene.

Don't be ridiculous, she thought, knowing he would never agree to it.

Lena drove a block over. She parked on a street near the back of the mountain trail and looked around. Aside from a few children playing in their front yards, no one was in the area.

She slowly climbed out of the car. A silver chain-link fence stood at the base of the mountain trail. The climb appeared a bit steep, but doable.

Okay, here goes nothing...

Lena jumped the fence. She steadied herself, digging her feet into the dirt while scaling the trail. Rogue tree roots and wild foliage grew from the dry, red earth. Lena grabbed hold of the shrubbery as she pulled her body up toward the hiking path.

When she neared the top of the foothill, Lena heard a commotion in the near distance. She paused. The voices were to her right. She jogged up to the path and dusted herself off, then set out in the direction of what she assumed was the crime scene.

Five minutes into the trail, Lena noticed red biohazard tape up ahead. It had been wrapped around several massive sequoia trees.

Law enforcement officers were swarming around the outer perimeter while only a few surveyed the area within the tape.

She stepped off the trail and crept closer to the scene, walking discreetly in between the tree trunks. As she searched the inner perimeter for David, Lena noticed the coroner kneeling down near the victim's body.

Tears flooded Lena's eyes as she watched him slip paper bags over the victim's hands and wrap them in tape. Her entire body trembled as the sight brought back haunting memories of the crime scenes back in LA.

"Did you get all of her clothing secured in the evidence bags?" she heard the coroner ask one of the officers.

Russ walked over toward him, carrying several brown paper bags. "I did, along with a few other items we're hoping will contain viable clues."

Lena craned her neck. She noticed Miles and Jake, walking along the outskirts of the crime scene tape with their flashlights focused on the ground.

I wanna get in there, she thought to herself.

Despite her brief moment of PTSD, she couldn't fight her desire to jump in and help. Lena felt as though this was her case to solve. Yet here she was, forced to take a back seat while her entire family worked the investigation without her.

Just as Lena noticed the coroner unfolding a linen sheet, David and her father approached him.

"Are you preparing to take the victim down to the morgue?" David asked him.

"I am. I've processed the body thoroughly, allocated an identifying number and had plenty of photos taken."

Lena watched as her father crossed his arms tightly over his chest. "All right then," he said just as two transporters walked over. One of them unzipped a body bag and placed it next to the victim.

Lena took a few steps closer, watching as the men carefully wrapped the victim in the sheet, then placed her inside of the bag.

"Chief!" Miles called out. "Can you and David come and take a look at this?"

"Be right over," Kennedy told him before turning back to the coroner. "We'll finish processing the scene while you begin the autopsy procedures. I'll be in touch soon."

"Sounds good, Chief Love."

Lena felt herself growing anxious. She stepped back and forth, contemplating her next move. When she did, dried leaves crackled underneath her sneakers. The noise caused the group to turn toward the trunk that Lena was hiding behind.

She ducked quickly, almost slamming her head against a thick branch in the process. She held her breath, waiting to see if someone would come over and investigate the noise. When they continued talking among themselves, Lena held her hand to her chest and slowly exhaled.

In that moment, she knew she had only two choices. Either approach the scene and ask if she could participate or go back home.

But then Lena thought back on the phone conversation she overheard her mother having with her father. He'd made it clear that he didn't want her to even know about the murder. There was no way he'd want her to get involved in the investigation.

Lena slowly turned around, her shoulders slumped in defeat. Then, as she crept back down the side of the trail toward her car, a thought crossed her mind.

She glanced back at the crime scene. David and her father were standing next to Miles and Jake, who were busy placing something inside an evidence bag.

You may not be able to get in there now. But you will...

LENA STARED UP at the sky. Lush layers of lavender, yellow and orange blended together, creating a beautiful backdrop. It was a complete contradiction of the bleak crime scene up ahead.

She gripped the handle on her forensic kit, then straightened her shoulders. As darkness began to fall over Clemmington, law enforcement had cleared the area where the victim had been murdered. Lena was there at the Juniper hiking trail alone.

She once again managed to elude the police officers who were standing guard at the trail's entryway by climbing up the back of the mountain. Now that she was standing on the outskirts of the red biohazard tape, adrenaline pulsated through her veins. The urge to dig into the scene and see what she could find began to overtake her.

Lena set her field kit down on the ground and pulled out a pair of booties. She slid them over her combat boots, then slipped on a pair of latex gloves and eye goggles.

She slowly approached the tape and stooped down, careful not to disturb it as she crept underneath and entered the killing ground. Lena pulled her flashlight from her pocket and shined it down on the dry, reddish-brown dirt. Her eyes were focused on the forest floor. She studied every rock, leaf and pine needle in search of the tiniest bit of evidence.

A few steps in, Lena noticed a small pool of dried blood that had soaked into the dirt. She quickly whipped open her kit and pulled out a metal scalpel. Lena dug the tool into the dirt, careful to pick up the scoop without disturbing the bloodstain. She then slipped it inside a paper evidence bag and stored it inside her case.

Lena stood up and continued on, moving carefully through every inch of the scene. When a gust of chilly wind blew open her suede navy jacket, she realized that the temperature was dropping. Lena quickly zipped the blazer and kept going.

The eerie sound of dried twigs crackling underneath her feet filled the air. Lena could feel her heart rate increasing. She was suddenly hit with flashbacks of being on that trail back in LA, surveying the scene alone before being attacked.

That was then, this is now, she told herself. *Press on toward the goal...*

Any remnants of overhead light were fading fast. But Lena intended on scouring the scene until there was nothing left to uncover.

Something flapping in the wind up ahead caught Lena's attention. It was outside the crime scene tape, stuck underneath a pile of leaves. She hurried over to the small heap, ducking underneath the tape and aiming the flashlight at the foliage.

A crackling tree limb snapped. Lena jumped up just as the large branch crashed to the ground.

She shrieked at the sight. Suddenly, Lena felt as though she was not alone.

Her entire body stiffened up. She held her breath, pushing thoughts of the killer lurking there out of her mind.

Calm down, she told herself, convinced that he

wouldn't be bold enough to return to the crime scene, especially knowing it was under police surveillance. Nevertheless, she kept her eyes glued to the tree, waiting for the killer to jump out at her.

The area remained motionless. No one appeared. Lena sighed with relief, realizing that she'd merely witnessed an innocent act of nature.

She turned her attention back to whatever was tucked underneath the leaves. Lena bent down again and began sifting through the pile. She grabbed hold of the material stuck at the bottom. When a black leather glove appeared, Lena almost fainted.

She tightened her lips before releasing a squeal of elation, then slipped the glove inside an evidence bag.

"What else can I find?" she whispered into the wind, forgetting all about the fallen tree branch that had terrified her moments ago.

Suddenly, the sky lit up. Flashes of lightning flickered within dark gray clouds. The roaring sound of thunder rippled through the air.

"You have *got* to be kidding me," Lena groaned.

Rain was not in the forecast. So she'd neglected to pack an umbrella.

"Let me hurry up so I can get out of here," she mumbled to herself.

Lena slid back underneath the crime scene tape and continued scouring the area.

She took a deep breath. The musky scent of an incoming storm filled the air. But as long as the rain remained at bay, she would stick to her mission.

The sky flashed with bright lightning. It lit up the

area around her. From the corner of her eye, Lena could've sworn she saw a shadowy figure, looming near the fallen tree branch.

She quickly swiveled her head. Darkness filled the air as the lightning subsided. When it flashed again, no one was there.

Your mind is playing tricks on you...

But then Lena heard footsteps creeping over the dried earth. She pivoted in a circle, shining her flashlight into the distance. Nothing but trees appeared. And then, silence.

Raindrops began to slide down her eye goggles, obscuring her vision.

You need to get the hell out of here. Now!

The thick, humid air fogged her lenses. She pulled the goggles off and shoved them inside her pocket. Her feet sank into the muddy ground as the rain went from a drizzle to a downpour.

Heavy droplets splashed against Lena's eyelids, further impairing her vision. She rushed away from the crime scene area and slipped off her booties.

Just as she reached the hiking trail, lightning illuminated the sky. A shadowy figure appeared before her.

Lena recoiled when he placed his hand on her shoulder. Before she could let out a scream, the man called out her name.

"What are you doing out here?" he yelled.

Lena moved in closer. She almost fell to her knees after realizing it was Officer Underwood.

"I—I wanted to search the area for clues," she stammered. "How did you know I was here?"

"Your mother called in to the police station and reported you missing. She figured we might find you at the crime scene."

The officer wrapped his arm around Lena and led her toward the hiking trail's entrance.

"Come on. Let's get you home."

Chapter Eleven

David parked his car in front of the Love family's house. He slowly stepped out and waved at the officer in the squad car across the street, then made his way toward the front door.

"Do not go off," he whispered to himself. "Stay calm. Keep your cool. Do not jump down this woman's throat. She's already been through enough."

But as the words came out of his mouth, David could feel streaks of anger churning inside his stomach. When he'd received the news late last night that Lena had been found investigating the Juniper hiking trail, he thought it was a joke. He just knew that she wouldn't step foot onto that crime scene.

Unfortunately, he'd been wrong.

You should have known better, David thought.

Lena had never been the type of woman who could be contained. When she wanted something, she went after it. Especially when it came to her career. And because she had such personal ties to this case, her passion to solve it ran deep.

"Deep enough for you to risk your own life," he muttered, shaking his head in disappointment.

David climbed the porch stairs and reached up to ring the doorbell. Just as his fingertip hovered over the button, Chief Love's loud voice boomed from inside the house.

"Lena, this is it!" Kennedy yelled. "I have *had* it with your erratic behavior! You going behind our backs and trying to solve this case on your own is not gonna cut it. Why would you go out and risk your life, *yet again*, like you're some damn superhero?"

"You're gonna mess around and give Mama a heart attack," David heard Jake chime in.

"Can everybody just please calm down for a minute?" Miles interjected.

David went ahead and rang the doorbell, figuring now was a good time to interrupt the heated exchange. Even though he was in full agreement with Kennedy and Jake, he didn't want to see everyone gang up on Lena.

"Coming!" David heard Mrs. Love call out. When she opened the door, he noticed her eyes were red and puffy, and her face was creased with worry.

"David, please, come in. I am so glad that you're here."

"Sounds like I'm walking into the middle of World War Three."

"You may as well be."

David stepped inside the living room where the Love family was holding court. Jake and Miles were sitting on the sectional, Lena was seated across them on the love seat and Kennedy was pacing the floor.

"Can I get you something to drink?" Betty asked David right before Kennedy threw his hands in the air.

"No, Miles!" he ranted. "I will not calm down. None of this would even be happening had your sister listened to her father, stayed in Clemmington and worked for our police force. But *no*. Rather than remain loyal to her family and her hometown, she chose to run to the big city and—"

"*Excuse* me," Betty interrupted. "We have company now. It would be nice if you all could show some civility toward one another."

The family turned toward David. From the looks on their surprised faces, they hadn't even noticed him enter the room.

"Hello, everyone," he said, nodding his head awkwardly.

The group fell silent. The tension in the air was apparent. David wondered if he should turn around and leave. It felt as though he was intruding on a private family matter.

Lena looked over at him. When he saw the pained expression on her tear-streaked face, his anger toward her immediately subsided.

She glanced around the room, then pointed at David. "Why did you all call him here? So you'd have yet another person on your team to jump down my throat?"

"No, Lena," Kennedy replied. "I've actually assigned David as the lead detective on this case. And Officer Campbell will be handling forensics."

She glared at David, clearly displeased with the news. The look in her eyes appeared as though she felt betrayed by him.

David watched as she sank down farther into the couch. Her slumped posture reeked of defeat. She stared down at her lap, fidgeting with the stray threads hanging from a beige throw pillow.

"Lena," Kennedy said, "why don't you tell David about the evidence you found out on the—"

Before he could finish, she jumped up from the couch.

"I can't do this," Lena insisted before storming out of the room.

Miles hopped up and went after her.

"Hold on," Kennedy called out to him. "Let her go. She probably needs a break from us. I think we all need to take a minute and cool down." He turned to David. "Would you mind going to check on her?"

"Of course not."

"Thank you," Betty whispered, giving his shoulder an appreciative pat.

David walked through the dining room and entered the kitchen, expecting to see Lena sitting at the table. But the room was empty. He walked over to the sliding glass doors and noticed her out on the deck, leaning against the wrought-iron table with her head in her hands.

He knocked on the glass to get her attention. She looked up, her watery eyes blinking rapidly as she stared at him. After a few moments she waved her hand, motioning for him to come outside.

David stepped out onto the deck and slowly approached her.

"You okay?" he asked.

"Not really."

"You wanna talk about it?"

"Not at all."

"Understood."

He walked around the table and sat down, stretching his legs out in front of him.

"You know," he began, "you've been through so much, Lena. Do you think you should talk to someone? A professional?"

"What, a *shrink*?" Lena snorted. "Absolutely not. With a job like mine, danger comes with the territory."

David felt that streak of anger return. He sat straight up in his chair and turned to her.

"Actually, it doesn't," he shot back. "Your job as a forensic investigator does not entail you roaming around taped off crime scenes, alone at night, leaving yourself vulnerable to being—"

"Um, *excuse* me, Detective Hudson," she interrupted, crossing her arms in front of her. "I don't need you telling me what my job entails. I am fully aware of the criteria and have quite a successful track record to prove it."

"No doubt. But clearly your judgment is questionable considering you were willing to put your life on the line to investigate a crime scene that we'd thoroughly processed."

David watched as Lena's lips curled into a smug smirk.

"Thoroughly processed, you say?" she asked.

His eyes lowered. He could sense that she was about to hit him with some surprising news.

"Judging by your silence," she continued, "you must not have heard about the evidence that I collected at the crime scene."

"No," he replied, shifting in his chair. "I didn't. Your family was so upset that you went out there by yourself that they didn't mention it."

"Well, thanks to *me*, there's a scoop of blood-soaked dirt and a leather glove down at the crime lab waiting to be processed. I'd like to examine the evidence myself, but my father insists on holding me captive here at the house."

"I'm not surprised that you found evidence everyone else overlooked. You're exceptional at what you do. And I'm sure the lab's facility director will prioritize processing it."

"My father already spoke to her. She said she would. But you know me. I'd rather process it myself."

"Of course you would. Your need to control is unwavering."

Lena turned away from David and stared out at the lawn. "So is my passion for my work. And my determination to solve this case."

Her steely expression silenced him. He knew from experience that once she shifted into go mode, there was no pulling her out of it.

Lena threw her head back and leaned against the railing. "I just wanna get out of here. I'm actually thinking about calling Chief Scott and talking to him about going back to LA. I'm ready to get back to work."

"That's it," David said. He jumped up from his chair and joined her over at the railing. When she ignored him, he leaned in and forced her to make eye contact.

"Lena, you do not, I repeat, *do not*, need to go back to work. The suspect is obviously following you. If he trails you back to LA, you already know the LAPD won't look after you the way your family would. The way *I* would. I think you need to stay put and let us protect you while we handle the investigation."

"But that's exactly what the killer would expect me to do," she replied. "Hide out here in my hometown, under the watch of my family. He'd never think that I would be bold enough to go back to LA. So while he's busy trying to catch up to me in Clemmington, I'll be back in the city, investigating the crime scenes in hopes of gathering more evidence."

"You have *got* to be kidding me," David grunted.

"Listen. I'm suffocating in this town. My father and brothers are smothering me to death. Every day I'm being reminded of why I didn't stay here and work for the Clemmington PD in the first place. I can't stand being treated like the baby of the family. I just want to do my job, catch this killer and get back to my life in Los Angeles."

David felt a piercing burn sear through his chest. He was quickly reminded of the moment all those years ago, when Lena graduated college and told him she wasn't moving back to Clemmington.

"This place has never been enough for you," he said,

thinking more of the people in it rather than the town itself. "And it obviously never will."

He stood there, waiting for Lena to tell him he was wrong. When she didn't, he turned around and headed back toward the house.

"I hope you'll reconsider going back to LA. Trust me, it's a bad idea."

"Wait, you're leaving?"

"Yes. I'm leaving. I've said my piece. You seem to have your mind made up on what you want to do. But like I said, I hope you'll reconsider."

Lena turned so quickly that her sneakers squeaked against the deck's slippery wood surface.

"I will," she said.

"You will what?"

"I'll reconsider. But on one condition."

David paused. His hand fell from the sliding door's handle.

"And what's that?" he asked.

"You'll talk to my father about letting me process that evidence I collected from the Juniper hiking trail myself."

David's head rolled in exasperation. "Why is that so important to you? Don't you trust that our lab can get the job done?"

"Of course I do," Lena insisted, walking over to him.

She stood so close that he could smell her vanilla-scented perfume floating through the air. Her soft expression dismantled his defensive stance. In that moment, he would've agreed to anything she wanted.

"Can I be honest with you?" she asked.

"Of course."

"Being stuck here inside my parents' house has made me feel...*useless*. To the point where I'm starting to question my own self-worth. Like, what's my purpose? I've worked so hard to get to where I am in my career, and the minute I start focusing on the investigation of a lifetime, *bam!* I'm forced off the case and relegated to the sidelines. That's pretty demoralizing, David."

David gently placed his hand on her shoulder. "But think about *why* you were taken off the case, Lena. No one is trying to strip you of your purpose. We all know how talented you are. We're just doing this to keep you safe."

"I know." She sighed. "And even though all that sounds perfectly reasonable, it still doesn't feel good. I can't stand the thought of being completely removed from this investigation. After all I've been through, *I* want to be the one to track down that son of a bitch."

David winced at the menacing anger in her low tone. As a member of law enforcement, he understood Lena's desire to finish what she'd started. Yet as a close friend, he wanted nothing more than to protect her.

"I'll tell you what," he said, slowly removing his hand from her shoulder. "I will see what I can do about getting you into the lab to process the evidence. Meanwhile, why don't we switch gears and drop the topic of the investigation for now? Maybe go inside and check on your family? They seemed pretty wound up when I first got here."

"To put it mildly."

When David threw her a look, Lena rolled her eyes.

"Fine," she groaned. "But only if a glass of wine is included in me walking back inside that house."

"I'm sure that can be arranged," he said. "And hey, you've gotta promise me that you won't go investigating another crime scene. Unless you've gotten the green light from law enforcement and are with the team, of course."

Lena turned to face him, her eyebrows furrowing in response to David's request.

"Let me hurry up and put in that call to my real boss back in LA," she quipped. "Because it sounds to me like somebody who I *don't* report to is trying to make demands."

The smirk on her face told David that she was just joking. But the fact that she didn't agree to his request left him feeling slightly worried.

Just let it go, he told himself. *For now...*

Chapter Twelve

The next morning, Lena stood at her bedroom window. She parted the curtains and stared out onto the street. The squad car that had become a permanent fixture on the block was parked in front of the house.

"Lena!" her mother called out. "I just brewed a fresh pot of coffee. Should I pour you a cup? Maybe make you an omelet—"

"No, thanks, Mom," Lena interrupted, her strained tone filled with frustration. "I'm working on something. I'll be out in a bit."

"Okay. I'm going out to run a few errands. Do you need anything?"

"Nope, I'm good. I'll see you when you get back."

Lena grabbed her cell phone. There were no new notifications. She pulled up the last text message that David had sent.

He'd received word from the forensics lab that the results were in on the evidence they'd collected at Nancy's Country Mart. The perpetrator's fingerprints and biological evidence did not match up with any of the offenders stored in the national DNA database.

The disappointing news left Lena feeling even more determined to catch the killer before he struck again.

Lena pulled up Chief Scott's phone number and called her boss back in LA. He picked up after the first ring.

"Chief Scott," he barked.

"Chief, it's your favorite forensic investigator."

"Lena! How are you doing?"

"Ah, I've been better. Let's just say that."

"Well, that's perfectly understandable," he replied quietly. "Things have been pretty brutal for you. You're a tough one, though. I will say that."

"Thanks, Chief. I'm trying to stay strong. This is what I signed up for when I decided to go into the criminal justice field, right?"

"Not necessarily. Your job is to collect and process evidence while law enforcement is on the scene. You shouldn't be subjected to safety issues. However, with that being said…"

Uh-oh, here we go, Lena thought, feeling as though she was talking to David all over again.

"Your safety never would've been jeopardized had you followed the rules and not visited that crime scene alone," Chief Scott continued.

"With all due respect, Chief, I didn't call you for a lecture."

"Then you shouldn't have called me at all. Because you know how I am. I will always be the one to put you in check over your rogue behavior."

Lena closed her eyes and pressed her fingertips against her forehead. "Trust me, you're not the only one. But listen. I'm growing more and more frustrated by the suspect. The way he's taunting me, all while he keeps getting away with murder. I'm beginning to feel as though his crime spree has turned into a personal vendetta against me."

"Rule number one when it comes to investigations is that you cannot take these cases personal. You have got to keep your head on straight and make good choices. Don't let the killer outsmart you. You're too skilled for that."

"The fact that the perp is trying to outsmart me is actually why I'm calling you," Lena said while sitting down on the side of the bed. "Now that we know he's on the hunt for me here in Clemmington, I think this would be the perfect time for me to come back to LA. I could reexamine the crime scenes there, try and collect more evidence and compare it to the DNA we recovered here in—"

"Whoa whoa whoa," Chief Scott interrupted. "You can stop right there. There's no way in hell I'd put you back on the job right now. Not after everything you've been through. I think you need to take more time to recuperate. I'd also advise you to talk to someone. We can connect you with a licensed trauma and PTSD therapist who would help…"

As the chief rambled on, Lena felt her jaws tighten. She resisted the urge to hang up on him. Nothing coming out of his mouth resonated with the way she was feeling, let alone how she wanted to proceed with the investigation.

"And when I spoke with your father last night,"

Chief Scott continued, "he made it clear that he did not want you returning to LA and getting back to work."

Lena jumped up and began pacing the floor. "Wait, you talked to my father?"

"Yes, I did. After he heard from one of his detectives that you mentioned coming back to LA to continue working on the case, he called me just to make sure we're all on the same page. Luckily, we are. The consensus is that you need to stay put."

"And let me guess. The detective who shared that information with my father was David Hudson?"

"Yeah, I believe that was his name."

Lena rushed over to her closet and pulled down a pair of jeans and a fitted yellow tunic.

"So will you consider talking to a therapist?" Chief Scott asked.

"I'll think about it," she huffed while throwing off her robe and stepping into her pants. "In the meantime, I'd better go. My mom made breakfast and she's waiting on me."

"All right. Well, thanks for calling. It's always good to hear from you. And, Lena? Please, do me a favor. Make good choices. And stay out of trouble."

"I'll do my best, Chief. Talk to you soon."

Lena disconnected the call and rushed into the bathroom. She quickly applied a light layer of makeup and ran a flat iron through her hair. After slipping on a pair of tan leather wedges, she grabbed her purse and sneaked out the back door.

LENA BURST INSIDE the police station and stormed up to Milly's desk.

"Where's Detective Hudson?" she snapped.

"Well, good morning to you, too," Milly replied, her eyes wide as she leaned back in her chair. "What in the world has gotten into you?"

"I'm sorry. I'm just pissed off. I need to speak with Detective Hudson. *Immediately*."

Milly pointed the long, purple acrylic nail of her index finger toward the back of the station.

"Check his office. Last time I saw him, he was headed that way with a pile of folders in one hand and a cup of coffee in the other."

"Thanks," Lena muttered.

She shot past the breakroom, noticing Russ and Officer Underwood standing near the vending machine. When she reached her father's office, she slowed down. Just as she inched toward the window and peeked inside, Milly yelled out her name.

"You're fine!" she told Lena. "Your father and brothers are back at the Juniper hiking trail where that poor woman was found murdered. They're giving it another look, just to make sure all of the evidence was collected."

I bet they are, after I recovered that glove, Lena thought to herself.

"Thanks, Milly!" she said before setting off toward David's office.

The door was closed. Lena wanted to kick it in after finding out he'd snitched on her. But instead she took a deep breath and knocked, albeit more aggressively than necessary.

"Come in!"

She grabbed the knob and swung the door open so forcefully that it slammed against the wall. David jumped back in his chair. His mouth fell open, and he stared at her as if he'd seen a ghost.

"Lena! What are you doing here? And how did you get here? Did the officer watching over the house escort you?"

"No, he did not. And before you get to lecturing me, let me ask you this. Why in the hell did you tell my father that I was thinking about going back to LA?"

David moaned loudly and stood up.

"Please. Have a seat," he told her while closing the door. "Can I get you anything? Coffee? Water?"

"Cut the niceties and answer my question. Why would you sell me out like that? I thought we were friends. You couldn't have kept that information to yourself?"

David walked back around the desk and sat down. He took a long sip of coffee, watching Lena closely as she took a seat across from him.

"Look," he said. "You don't listen to me. And you going back to LA right now is a terrible idea. So I did what I had to do to stop it from happening."

"You are aware that you nor my father have that much power and control over me, aren't you? I can come and go as I please."

"Lena, this is not about power or control. Again, this is about your safety. It's just a shame that we're all more concerned about that than you." David paused and shook his head. "I really believed that getting you back inside the crime lab would've been enough to pacify you. At least for the time being. I guess I was wrong."

"Wait, what are you talking about?"

"Didn't you get my text message?" he asked.

"No," she mumbled while scrambling around inside her purse. "I was so angry after talking to Chief Scott that I hadn't checked my phone."

David sat up straighter in his chair. "Well, I talked to your father this morning and asked if he'd be willing to let you process the evidence you retrieved from the Juniper hiking trail."

"You—you did?" she asked, blinking rapidly as if she hadn't quite comprehended what he'd just said.

"I did."

"But why?"

"Because I know how much it means to you. And I understand how you feel. About everything. I don't want to see you be completely removed from the investigation. So, after wearing your father down for almost thirty minutes, I finally got him to agree to let you inside the lab."

A slight smile spread across Lena's lips.

"Thank you for doing that, David. It means a lot knowing that *someone* gets how I feel."

"You're welcome," he said, grabbing his keys and wallet. "So, now that we've gotten all that straightened out, should we head to the lab?"

"Yes!" Lena exclaimed.

She hopped up from her chair and ran around the desk, throwing her arms around David. When he returned the hug, she turned her head and kissed him square on the lips.

"Oops!" Lena squealed, jumping back and covering her mouth. "I am so sorry. I—I don't know what got into me. I just—I guess I was just…"

"Too excited to contain yourself?" he asked, chuckling as he headed toward the door. "No worries. I'll chalk it up as your way of giving thanks. Now come on. Let's get out of here."

Lena dropped her head, mortified by her actions but grateful that he'd made light of the situation.

But when she glanced over at David, Lena noticed an intensity in his gaze that appeared far from nonchalant.

Chapter Thirteen

David held the door open for Lena as they exited the crime lab.

"Whew!" She sighed, bouncing down the stairs. "That felt good. Really good. I can't thank you enough for talking my father into letting me process the evidence, David."

"Don't mention it. That's the least I could do, especially considering you were the one who retrieved it from the crime scene. I still don't understand how all of Clemmington PD managed to overlook it."

Lena gave him a wink and dusted off her shoulders. "Hey, what can I say. I'm just that good."

"Oh *really*. Is that what it is?"

"That's exactly what it is."

David couldn't help but smile at her upbeat demeanor. Despite her most recent attack, he was glad to see she was in better spirits. It reassured him that he'd done the right thing by talking her father into letting her analyze the evidence.

Lena turned to him as they headed toward his car. "Hey, I've been meaning to ask you something. Was the woman who was murdered on the Juniper hiking trail ever identified?"

"Yes, she was. Her name was Ashley Duncan. What's strange is that she wasn't a Clemmington resident. She actually lived a couple of towns over, in Valley Oak."

David noticed Lena's pace slow down a bit. When they reached his car, she fell against the passenger door.

"Are you okay?" he asked.

"I'm—I'm fine," she breathed while holding her hand to her chest. "I just… I wonder if the suspect kidnapped her in Valley Oak, then assaulted her here in Clemmington, just to torment me."

David had already taken that theory into consideration. But he didn't mention it to Lena for fear of stressing her out even further.

"Well, the good news is the lab director promised to have the DNA results back on the evidence you just processed within the next week or so," he said in an attempt to steer the conversation in a positive direction. "Hopefully that'll bring us even closer to arresting the perp."

"Hopefully…" Lena mumbled, her wavering tone less than confident.

"Come on. Be optimistic. We're getting closer and closer every day, and—"

David was suddenly interrupted by a woman's voice.

"Lena? Lena Love?" she called out.

He turned around and noticed a thin, dark-haired woman walking toward them.

"Katie?" Lena called out. "Hey, girl!"

David looked on as the woman ran over, embracing Lena tightly.

"How are you?" Lena asked her. "What are you doing here in this neck of the woods?"

"I'm doing well. I actually just started working here at the lab as a forensic scientist."

"*Really?* Oh, wow, congratulations!"

Lena clutched the woman's arm and turned to David.

"David, this is Katie Winters. She and I attended Pacific Western University together. Katie, meet David Hudson. He's a detective with the Clemmington PD."

"It's nice to meet you, Katie," he said, reaching out and shaking her hand. "Congratulations on the new job."

"Thank you so much. It's nice to meet you, as well."

Katie turned back to Lena and gently placed her hands on her shoulders.

"How are you doing?" she asked softly. "I was so sorry to hear about what happened to you back in LA."

"I'm hanging in there. David and I were actually here processing evidence that I collected from the most recent crime scene in Clemmington."

Katie's hands fell down by her sides as she shook her head. "I can't believe that bastard committed another murder, right in your hometown. It's as if he's following you. I pray you all get him behind bars before he strikes again."

"That's exactly what we're working to do," David told her.

"Good," Katie responded. "Well, I'd better get back to work. My lunch break ended fifteen minutes ago. I'd hate to get fired during my first week on the job. David, it was great meeting you, and, Lena, it was wonderful seeing you. We have got to keep in touch. Is your contact information the same?"

"It is. I'd love to get together and catch up."

"Same here. I'll be in touch soon."

Lena waved goodbye, then turned to David.

"That was so nice, running into her," she said as they climbed inside the car. "It'll be good to reconnect with someone from college who's in the same line of work as me."

"I'm sure it will be," David replied while driving out of the parking lot. "But you best believe that if you two decide to get together, you'll be chaperoned."

"Oh *God*," Lena groaned. "Are you serious? I feel like a kid all over again."

"Remember, safety first. So listen. I'll take you back to the police station to pick up your car, then follow you back to your parents' house. You know, just in case…"

"I know. Just in case the killer is following me."

David noticed a mist in Lena's eyes as she stared straight ahead. He reached over and nudged her thigh.

"I tell you what," he began. "After I get off work tonight, why don't we go out to dinner? And I don't mean a quick, casual meal. I'm talking suit and tie, fancy dress and high heels type of dinner. How does that sound?"

Lena nodded her head and forced a smile. "That

sounds amazing, actually. And much needed. Thank you."

"You're welcome. I figured you'd enjoy doing something nice that would break up the monotony of dealing with this investigation."

"I definitely would. Looking forward to it."

"So am I."

"MMM, THIS IS really good," David said. He slid his plate of dark chocolate ganache tart across the table toward Lena. "Here, try it. You'll love it."

"I can't," she moaned. "I am stuffed. I ate way too much of my blueberry lavender cheesecake."

"So what are you saying?" David asked as he emptied a bottle of Riesling into their glasses. "You didn't leave room to finish off this delicious wine?"

"I didn't say all that now," Lena protested before they broke out into laughter.

David took a sip of his wine while staring across the table at her. Lena looked beautiful dressed in a black slip minidress and silver kitten heel pumps. She'd pulled her hair into a sophisticated chignon, which highlighted her sparkling dangle earrings and matte red lipstick perfectly.

David had reached into the back of his closet and pulled out one of his better dark gray suits, which he'd paired with a crisp white shirt and pink silk tie. But all eyes were inevitably on his stunning companion.

"I've had such a great time tonight," Lena told him. "I haven't had this good of a time in…"

When her voice trailed off, he gave her a flirtatious wink.

"In a long time?" he asked.

"A *really* long time. I don't want the night to end."

"It doesn't have to."

Lena tilted her head. "Meaning?"

"Meaning we could take this back to my place. Listen to some music. Crack open the bottle of Cabernet Sauvignon reserve wine that I've been saving for a special occasion."

David's mind inadvertently drifted to the moment in his office earlier that day when Lena kissed him. He wondered if they would pick up where they'd left off later.

"So you consider tonight a special occasion?" she asked.

"I most certainly do."

Lena dabbed the corners of her mouth with her napkin and picked up her clutch. "Okay then. Let's go."

David paid the check, then led her out of the restaurant. When she intertwined her arm with his, he was hit with a bout of nostalgia. David felt as though they were back in high school, and he was once again dating the most popular girl in class.

The pair climbed inside the car. Just as he started the engine, his cell phone buzzed loudly against the dashboard.

"No, don't answer it," Lena said. "I do not want our wonderful evening being interrupted by any nonsense."

"Neither do I. But unfortunately, I've got to check it. Could be an emergency."

David tapped his phone's home screen and opened the new notification.

"This is your father texting me," he said.

"What does that nosy man want?" Lena asked. "He knows we're out at dinner."

"Maybe he just wants to check in and make sure I'm behaving myself," David joked as he began reading the message.

Get down to Roble Park immediately! We've got another murder on our hands. Female victim, strangled to death with a heart carved into her chest. She was new to town. Worked at the forensics lab. She's been identified as Katie Winters.

A freezing chill swept over David. His mouth fell open and immediately went dry.

Lena turned to him and grabbed his arm.

"Hey, what's wrong? Are you okay?"

"Uh—I…"

He was too stunned to speak. So he handed Lena his phone so that she could read the message for herself.

After a few seconds, she let out a guttural scream.

"I am so sorry, Lena," David said before slamming his foot against the accelerator and speeding off toward Roble Park.

Chapter Fourteen

Lena's entire body trembled with shock as she stepped carefully over the park's dried dirt trail. She and David hadn't had time to stop and change before rushing to the crime scene. Thankfully, he had a silver windbreaker and shoe covers stored in his car that she was able to slip over her dress and heels.

When Lena laid eyes on the wooded area up ahead, her muscles tensed. The sight of yellow caution tape wrapped around massive sycamore tree trunks brought back memories of her most recent attack.

Do not break down, she told herself, knowing this moment could lead to her being put back on the investigative team.

Despite being traumatized by her own experience, she was devastated that her friend had been killed and more determined than ever to catch the killer.

"Are you sure you're okay being here?" David asked, as if he'd read her mind.

"Honestly? I'm a bit shaken up. I can't believe Katie was killed. I mean, what's the likelihood that a personal friend of mine who just got to town, who I just so happened to see earlier today, is now dead? That's no coincidence."

"Yeah, I don't think so, either. I just hope your father doesn't reprimand me for bringing you out here."

"I'm sure he won't. He knew we were out together. You had no choice but to bring me considering you needed to get down here ASAP."

"That's true. And if he does say anything, that'll be my argument."

Lena glanced over at David. He was staring straight ahead, the corners of his mouth curled into a slight frown. When he began cracking his knuckles and quickening his pace, she broke out into a slow jog in an effort to keep up with him.

"Hey," she said, reaching over and gently placing her hand on his arm. "Are *you* okay?"

"I'm good," he barked. "Just ready to get to work."

Lena winced at the sound of his gruff tone. It was apparent that he was feeling the pressure to solve the case, especially now that he'd been named lead detective.

"We're going to get through this, David," she said, despite her own feelings of fear and doubt. "Together."

"Thanks," he replied quietly, covering her hand with his. "I needed to hear that. Now, let's see what we've got here."

The pair approached the crime scene tape. The area had been lit up with portable telescoping pole lights. Law enforcement officers were covered in hazmat suits, latex gloves and eye goggles. Lena could barely make out who was who.

David, who had already removed his suit jacket and tie, rolled up his sleeves.

"Hey!" he called out. "Where's Detective Campbell?"

"Right here!" Russ responded, waving his hand before walking over. He was carrying a black case in one hand and brown paper evidence bags in the other.

"You got a couple of extra hazmat suits?" David asked him.

"I do. They're in my other bag. I'll go and grab them." Russ paused, eyeing David and Lena from head to toe. "You two look awfully dressed up. Where are you coming from?"

"Not now, Campbell," David grunted. "Can you please just bring us those hazmat suits?"

"Sure, man," he replied while slowly backing away. "No need to get all huffy. It was just a question."

"Leave it to Russ to be worried about what we're doing while he's in the middle of a murder scene," Lena muttered under her breath.

"I know, right?" David said. "He's a good detective and all, but he is messy as hell. Gossips more than kids in high school."

Lena crossed her arms in front of her and stood on her tippy-toes. She craned her neck, struggling to see over the heads of the officers who were hovering near Katie's body. When she caught a glimpse of her friend's bare leg, Lena cringed and turned away.

She took several deep breaths and fanned her face. *Do not start panicking out here in front of all these officers.*

"Are you all right?" David asked her.

"I'm fine." She sniffed, quickly wiping away a few tears that had managed to escape from her eyes.

"Hey, you two asked for a couple of hazmat suits?"

Lena looked up and saw Miles approaching them with the protective gear in hand.

"We did," David said. "Russ couldn't bring them over to us himself? He had to recruit you to do it instead?"

"You know how he is. He claimed the chief asked him to finish processing the scene."

"Yeah, right," David muttered. He took the suits from Miles and handed one to Lena. "That dude is a trip."

Miles pointed over at her.

"Hey, does Dad know you're here?"

"I don't know," she said while quickly slipping on the coverall. "But he knew David and I were out at dinner, and told him to get down here immediately. So, he had no choice but to bring me."

"Well, are you okay with being here?" Miles asked. "Because, I mean… I know that Katie was your former classmate and friend. And I was thinking that the killer may have…"

"Murdered her to send me a message?" Lena asked after his voice faded. "The thought of that chills me to the core, Miles. Knowing he probably followed us to the lab and saw me talking to Katie, then hunted her down and killed her, is devastating. But it also makes me want to go even harder. So let's get to it."

"Let's get to what?" Lena heard someone ask behind her.

She turned around and saw her father approaching them.

"Get to *what*?" Chief Love repeated.

"I thought I could step in and help out with the investigation," Lena finally replied.

"The hell you can. I'm sorry, but I am not about to let you subject yourself to this case. Not after what you've been through. I've got Detective Campbell handling the forensics. Now, you can stick close by until I'm able to free someone up who'll take you back home. Until then, no investigative work for you."

"But, Dad, I—"

"Chief Love," Russ interrupted, "I could actually use some help processing the scene. I'm done collecting evidence from the body, and the medical examiner is on his way for the removal."

When Russ glanced over at Lena, she mouthed the words *thank you*, then turned to her father.

"See, Dad? Detective Campbell needs my assistance. Now that Katie's body has been processed and she'll be taken to the morgue, the hard part is over. Please, let me help handle the rest."

Chief Love glared at his daughter, his forehead creased with doubt.

"I don't like this," he stated. "I don't like it at all."

The chief paused, watching Lena closely. She stood firm, like a soldier at attention in front of her drill sergeant. When she didn't break, he turned to Russ.

"You'd better keep a close eye on her," Chief Love

said. "If you see any signs of distress, you pull her off the scene immediately. Am I clear?"

"Absolutely, sir."

Chief Love gave Lena one last look before turning to David.

"Detective Hudson, you come with me. I want to talk to you and Jake about a strategy on how we should be canvassing the town in search of this psychopath."

"Yes, sir," David responded.

When he walked past Lena, he threw her a look of caution, then turned his attention to Russ. The scowl on David's face said it all. He did not want her working one-on-one with Detective Campbell.

"Is there a problem?" Russ asked David before handing Lena a pair of gloves. He didn't wait for David to reply. Instead, Russ wrapped his arm around Lena's shoulders and led her toward the middle of the crime scene.

She could feel David's intense stare burning into her back as they walked away. But at this point, Lena wasn't concerned with either of the detectives' petty schoolboy antics. She'd shifted into forensic investigator mode and was ready to dig into the crime scene.

"What do we know so far?" she asked Russ. "Other than the fact that the victim was strangled to death and had a heart carved into her chest?"

"Her hands were tied behind her back."

"With what sort of ligature?"

"A three-strand twisted rope."

"That's my killer's modus operandi," Lena said. "Have you collected the rope?"

"I have. Along with blood evidence and photographs of a shoe print I found in the dirt near the body."

Russ handed Lena a flashlight. As they approached the body bag, she squeezed the light's handle and stared down at it, fumbling with the switch as if she were having trouble turning it on.

"You need help with that?" Russ asked.

"Nope," Lena insisted, a slight quaver in her voice. She tapped her chest with her fist and cleared her throat. "I've got it."

"The body bag has been zipped up and secured," he said gently. "So you don't have to worry about seeing your friend. And by the way, I'm so sorry that this happened to her. I'm sorry that *all* of this is happening, to you and the rest of the victims."

"Thanks, Russ. I appreciate you saying that."

"Of course. Look, I know I've got a…a *reputation* when it comes to the ladies. But I do have a heart."

"I know you do."

As the pair fell silent, Lena heard a commotion behind her. She turned around and saw the medical examiner and his team approaching the scene.

"Oh, good." Lena sighed, relieved that Katie's body was being removed.

Russ waved them over. After they greeted one another and the coroner took over, the detective grabbed Lena's hand and pulled her away.

"You doing okay?" he asked.

"Yes. I'm fine."

"Good. And you're still up for searching the area for more evidence?"

"Of course. Let's do it."

Russ tightened his grip on her hand. "All right then. Let's check out this spot over here," he suggested, leading her toward a taped-off corner. "I haven't examined it yet."

On the way there, Lena felt eyes on her. She looked up and saw David glaring at them.

She quickly snatched her hand out of Russ's grip. But it was too late. David had already seen them.

"OKAY, TEAM, I think we've got everything we need," Chief Love announced. "Let's wrap it up and get out of here."

Lena closed her eyes and pressed the back of her hand against her damp forehead.

"I am exhausted," she said, sighing. "What do you think? Do we have enough viable evidence here to formulate a solid DNA profile?"

"I think so," Russ confirmed. He secured the latch on his forensic case, then let out a huge yawn. "*Whew!* I guess I'm tired, too. But after this long, insane day, I could go for a drink. How about you? Wanna stop by Lacey's for a cocktail? Or two?"

"And fall asleep on you at the bar? I don't think so."

"Aw, come on. It's just a drink among friends. Plus we haven't had a chance to catch up since you've been back in town."

"Well, considering the fact that I'm pretty much in the witness protection program at the Love residence, I haven't been doing much socializing."

"It certainly looked like you were out getting your

mingle on with David before you two got here. I peeped the little black dress and silver shoes underneath the windbreaker and shoe covers."

"Wow, aren't you the observant one," Lena quipped.

"It's hard not to notice a woman as beautiful as you. But anyway, let me stop before I say too much. If I can't take you out for a drink, at least let me give you a ride home."

"I, um… I think that I should probably—"

Before Lena could finish, David came storming over.

"Are you ready to go?" he asked her gruffly.

"Yes. I am. Hey, are you oka—"

"I'm fine," he grunted before she could finish. "Just tired and anxious to get the hell out of here."

Lena stood awkwardly between the two men as they stared one another down. She writhed her hands before turning to Russ.

"I'm going to head out with David. Thanks for letting me join in on the investigation."

"Anytime. I'll be in touch regarding the evidence we collected. Maybe we can take it down to the crime lab together. Then finally grab that drink."

Lena peeked over at David. If looks could kill, Russ would be a dead man.

"Okay then, talk to you soon," she told Russ without addressing the crime lab or the invitation for drinks.

"Are you coming, or do you wanna meet me at the car?" David snapped.

"I'm coming."

He spun around and stormed away from the crime scene. Lena hurried after him.

They walked to the car in silence. David popped open the trunk and pulled out a plastic garbage bag. He and Lena removed their protective gear and stuffed it all inside. He tossed the bag into the trunk, slammed the lid shut, then threw open the passenger door.

"Why are you so angry?" she asked him.

"I'm not angry. I already told you, I'm tired."

"Do you still want to go back to your place and have that glass of wine?"

David shook his head. "It's been a long night, Lena. I think I'd better take you home."

The rejection caused her heart to pound so hard that it bounced up into her throat. She swallowed hard and slid inside the car.

David slammed the door and climbed into the driver's seat. Without saying a word, he started the engine and sped off.

Lena felt her body heating up as she seethed with anger.

"I cannot believe you're taking Russ's actions out on me. Especially after my friend was just killed and I helped to investigate the crime scene."

David remained silent for several moments before finally speaking up.

"I'm sorry. I just—I can't stand to see you fraternizing with him. He is such a womanizer. And I know exactly what he's trying to do."

"First of all, I wasn't fraternizing with Russ. I was taking care of business tonight. Secondly, I know exactly what he's trying to do, too. And I'm not giving in to it. So don't worry. I have no interest in socializing with your apparent enemy."

"He's not my enemy. He just isn't someone I want you associating with."

The tense exchange was interrupted when Lena's cell phone buzzed. She pulled it from her clutch.

A text message notification appeared on the screen. It was sent from an anonymous number.

She was immediately overcome by a sick feeling. Her hand shook as she opened the text.

Nine Ten I Struck Again…

The phone fell from her hand. She turned to David. "We've got bigger things to worry about than Russ."

Chapter Fifteen

David sat across from Lena at her parents' dining room table. She shuffled through the lab reports, comparing the results from all of the crime scene evidence.

"So the DNA profiles on every sample that we've processed match up," Lena said.

"Yes, they do."

"Which means that we're dealing with one killer. Not a copycat killer."

"Exactly."

"But the killer's profile didn't match anyone's DNA record in the CODIS criminal justice database?"

David sat back and folded his hands behind his head. "Unfortunately, no. It didn't. But at least it's been confirmed that a copycat killer doesn't exist. There's only one person who's been committing these murders."

"Right," Lena said before slamming the reports down onto the table. "But where do we go from here? This is so frustrating."

"I know it is. And I've been thinking about the next steps. This killer that we're dealing with has continuously stayed two steps ahead of us. We've gotta take a risk here. Do something unexpected. Set up a trap that'll catch him off guard in hopes that he'll make a mistake."

"That sounds good. Do you have a plan in mind?"

"No." David sighed. "Not yet. But we need to figure something out. Fast."

Lena grabbed her laptop and opened the lid. "Okay, let's just start brainstorming. Anything that comes to mind, I'll write it down. Then we'll go through everything, keep the good stuff and throw out whatever doesn't work."

"All right. Let's do it."

Betty walked into the room carrying a charcuterie board in one hand and a pitcher of iced tea in the other.

"How's it going in here?" she asked. "Anything insightful coming from those reports?"

"It would be if the suspect's profile matched up with someone's in the criminal database," Lena said. "But it doesn't."

"Oh, that's a bummer." Betty placed the board and pitcher down onto the table, then paused. "Wait, wouldn't that mean the killer has never been convicted of a crime?"

"It would," David confirmed. "Which is crazy. How could someone go from never being arrested to committing all of these brutal attacks?"

"Exactly," Betty replied, slowly shaking her head.

Lena turned to her mother. "But David and I are going to shift gears. We're working on a plan that'll hopefully beat him at his own game."

"Oh, really? Well, good. I'm looking forward to hearing all about it. And on that note, I'll leave you two alone so you can get back to work. Enjoy the snacks and tea."

"Mmm, we will," David said. "Thank you."

As soon as Betty was out of earshot, David grabbed Lena's hand.

"I just thought of something."

"Okay," she said while filling their glasses with tea. "What've you got?"

"Don't faint when you hear this, but what if you go back to LA?"

The pitcher almost fell from Lena's hand. David jumped up and grabbed it, setting it back down onto the table.

"I'm sorry," she said. "But weren't you the same guy who threw a fit when I mentioned going back to LA?"

"Hold on," David replied. "Just hear me out. This is different. We'd technically be using you as a pawn. *No offense,*" he quickly added when she threw him a look. "Listen, the bottom line is, if you go back to LA, the killer will follow you there. We could have you re-visit the crime scene out on the Cucamonga Wilderness hiking trail. The suspect will think you're alone, combing the area for additional evidence. But we'll have law enforcement in place, ready to apprehend him the minute he appears."

David waited for Lena to respond. She remained silent, her eyes focused on the charcuterie board rather than him. He leaned in, noticing her fallen expression.

"I'm sorry," he uttered. "That was too much to ask. And insensitive to suggest. I shouldn't have even—"

"I'll do it," Lena interrupted.

"You will?" David asked, watching as her eyes flickered with determination. "Are you sure?"

"Yes. I'm positive. I can't stand the thought of the killer murdering another innocent victim. So if we have to use me as bait in order to track him down, then so be it."

David paused. Lena was now focusing on the pepperoni slices she was placing on their saucers. Her calm demeanor was almost frightening.

"I see you watching me from the corners of your eyes," she said. "Trust me. I'm down with your idea. I know that between the Clemmington PD and the LAPD, I'll be fully protected."

"Of course you will be—"

Before David could finish, Betty came storming into the room.

"Excuse me, but you two will do no such thing!" she insisted, throwing a stack of napkins down onto the table. "Have you both completely lost your minds?"

"Mom, please," Lena said. "You didn't hear the whole conversation. Plus David and I haven't even put a solid plan in place yet. We're just throwing around ideas."

"First of all, I stood my nosy self right outside that doorway and heard every bit of your conversation. Second of all, no matter what type of plan you two put in place, the whole idea is utterly senseless. *Period.* Third of all—"

Betty was interrupted when Kennedy, Jake and Miles came bursting through the front door and into the dining room.

"Dude!" Jake yelled, shoving Miles's shoulder. "Do you know how ridiculous you sound right now? Smoky Pit does not have the best ribs in town. That would be Leon's Barbecue."

"Man, get outta here," Miles replied, shoving him back before approaching the table and rubbing his hands together. "Mmm, what do we have here? A little Brie and Parmesan, with a side of prosciutto and salami, along with a variety of other meats and cheeses?"

When he reached for the board, Betty slapped his hand away.

"Go wash your hands first," she commanded. "But before you do that, I need for all three of you to talk some sense into Lena and David."

"Uh-oh," David muttered as he slid down in his chair.

Kennedy walked over to Betty and planted a kiss on her forehead.

"Is it just me," he began, "or does this moment remind you of the good ole days, back when we still had a house full of kids and their friends?"

"I wish this moment reminded me of the good ole days," Betty muttered. "Go on, you two," she continued, pointing over at Lena and David. "Tell Chief Love about your brilliant little plan to catch the killer."

David noticed Jake walk over to his parents and stand next to Kennedy. He crossed his arms over his chest while looking down his nose at him and Lena.

Miles on the other hand stood near his sister, propping his hand against the back of her chair protectively. The lines of allegiance were clear.

David glanced over at Lena. Judging by the look of her downturned lips, she wanted no part of sharing their plan with her family. So he cleared his throat and began explaining the situation.

"Lena and I were going over the killer's DNA results, and discussing how frustrated we are that they didn't match anyone's in CODIS. Without any new and viable leads, we're convinced that the suspect will continue to get away with murder."

Kennedy glanced down at his watch, then back up at David. His right eyebrow shot up toward his forehead. "Um, Detective? Would you mind getting to the punch line? I've had a long day, and I can smell my wife's short ribs simmering in the Crock-Pot. I'm ready to *eat*."

Lena emitted a loud sigh and threw up her hands. "Long story short, David and I were thinking that we could set up some sort of sting operation. I would bait the killer to a certain location, and law enforcement would be there lying in wait."

Betty turned to Kennedy and nudged his arm.

"Can you believe what you're hearing right now?" she asked him. "They want to go back to LA so that the suspect will follow Lena, then lead him to the crime scene where Lena was first attacked."

Jake groaned loudly, slapping his palm against his forehead. "*Really?* Are you two being serious right now? That has got to be the dumbest idea I've ever heard. Lena, why would you want to subject yourself to being attacked yet again? You're not a cat. You don't have nine lives. Keep this up and the third time just might be the charm for the killer—"

"Come on, Jake," Miles interjected. "That's enough. I actually don't think it's a bad idea. Could it be dangerous? Yes. But if the plan is executed properly, we could very well capture the suspect."

"Well, like I said," Betty began, turning to Kennedy, "I think it's utterly senseless. Between the Clemmington PD and the LAPD, we've got two of the best law enforcement agencies on the case. Why put my child in the middle of the investigation and jeopardize her life?"

"Because nothing else we've tried has worked so far," Kennedy replied.

Everyone in the room turned to the chief, their mouths falling open in simultaneous shock.

"So what are you saying?" Betty asked. "That you're okay with this…this awful, dangerous idea?"

"I'm not saying that I'm okay with it. But I am saying that it's worth considering."

Betty turned away from her husband and stared down at the floor. She pressed her fingertips against her temples and massaged them vigorously.

"Okay," she whispered, "I see you've completely lost the script, as well. I'd better go check on my short ribs before I say something I might regret."

"Yeah," Jake said, his arms falling down by his sides, "I'd better go with you."

Once he and Betty were out of earshot, Kennedy approached the table.

"Listen," he said, "I think you two may be onto something. But let's drop it for now and reconvene tomorrow down at the station. Betty doesn't fully understand the pressure that we're under to get this case solved. So we shouldn't continue the conversation here at the house."

"Understood, sir," David replied. "Thank you for hearing us out."

"Yes, Dad," Lena added, "I really appreciate that."

"You're welcome. See? I'm not always the stern, strict tyrant that you make me out to be."

Lena laughed and nudged Miles's arm. "Maybe not today…"

Miles nodded his head in agreement, then turned to their father.

"But what about Jake?" he asked. "We need for him to get on board with this, too."

"Let me talk to him," the chief replied. "He'll come around. In the meantime, why don't you three start quietly brainstorming some specific ideas and taking notes? The better the plan, the faster he'll agree. Once we have a solid strategy, I'll put in a call to the LAPD's Chief Scott and run it by him."

"That sounds good," Lena said. "I'm so glad we're in the state of California. Since the suspect committed all of these crimes within state lines—"

"Clemmington PD is allowed to make an arrest anywhere in California, by law," Miles chimed in.

Kennedy walked over and shook his son's shoulder.

"Hey, look who's been brushing up on the criminal justice system's laws and procedures. Is that a promotion I see in your future?"

"*Very near* future," Miles responded with a huge grin.

"Keep this up and we just might bring that to fruition. But as for the *immediate* future, let's go check on your mother and brother and make sure they haven't disowned us. David, are you staying for dinner?"

"From the smell of those short ribs, I would love to. But I don't know. Mrs. Love may not want me here after that exchange we just had."

"Aw, don't worry about her. You're like family. She'll get over it just like she does whenever one of her own kids upsets her."

"Thank you, sir."

Once Kennedy and Miles left the room, David turned to Lena.

"Wow," he breathed. "That was intense. I'm actually sweating."

"*You're* sweating. I'm pretty sure my blood pressure is at stroke level. But the good news is, we accomplished our mission. I think this is it, David. If we come up with the right plan, we'll finally capture that son of a bitch."

David took a long sip of tea, then rolled up his sleeves.

"I agree. Now that the room has cleared out, let's dig into this cheese board and start thinking of a master plan."

Chapter Sixteen

NEWS RELEASE
Tuesday, August 10, 2021
Los Angeles Law Enforcement Media Relations

FORENSIC INVESTIGATOR LENA LOVE RETURNING TO WORK

Los Angeles: We are pleased to announce that our lead forensic investigator, Lena Love, will be rejoining the Los Angeles Police Department, effective immediately. Love had fallen victim to an attack that we believe was committed by a California serial killer. After returning to her hometown to recuperate with family, she feels ready to get back to work and continue lending her expertise to the department.

Love will be working part-time, primarily inside the forensics laboratory, as she eases back into her routine. Love's crime scene investigations will recommence at her discretion.

The LAPD continues to pursue the suspect, who is still at large. Anyone with information regarding this case is urged to contact the LAPD's Homicide Division. Anyone wishing to remain anonymous should call Crime Stoppers, or submit tips online.

Lena read through the press release one last time, then looked over at David.

"I think this sounds great," she said, spinning her laptop toward him. "What do you think?"

"I agree," he replied. "For the *fourth* time. Trust me. The LAPD's media relations department did an excellent job on the fake release. I definitely think it'll throw the killer off and convince him that you're back at work in LA."

"Awesome. I'm taking your word for it."

Lena composed an email to the public relations director, giving her the thumbs-up on the release. After cc'ing Chief Scott, she sent the message, then closed her computer.

"All right." She sighed, standing up and stretching her limbs. "Step one of the plan is in motion. What do you say we celebrate with a second glass of wine?"

"I'd say I like where your head's at. Let's do it."

Lena picked up their glasses and headed into her LA loft's sleek white kitchen. Two weeks had passed since they'd planned out their sting operation. She and David had arrived in town early that morning, just before sunrise. He'd offered to stay in a nearby hotel, but Lena insisted she'd feel more comfortable if he stayed with her. David agreed, and she set him up in her guest room.

Lena hadn't cohabitated with a man for an extended amount of time in years. She couldn't deny the fact that having David there felt good.

"So, when is the press release going to go live on the LAPD's website?" he asked.

"According to the PR director, as soon as she gets my approval. My guess is that the minute she sees my email, it'll be posted. Local news stations are going to share the news with the public, as well."

"And then, it'll be showtime. I'm sure our suspect will immediately leave Clemmington and head back to LA. Then when he comes for you, we'll come for him, and that'll be the end of this nightmare."

"From your lips to God's ears," Lena replied. "I can only hope it'll be that easy."

David propped his arms along the back of her gray suede couch and glanced around the living room.

"I love your place," he said. "The aesthetic is really cool. The high ceilings, exposed copper pipes, brick walls, and wide-open floor plan give it a bit of an industrial feel. Then your contemporary furnishings and artwork offer up a really slick, modern look."

Lena leaned back and stared across her marble island. "Listen to you, sounding like you write for *Elle Decor*. Thank you." She refilled their glasses with Pinot Noir rosé, then took a seat next to David. "I have yet to see your house. I bet it looks good."

"Ah, it's okay. Just a simple, rustic, trilevel townhome. Nothing too fancy. But I'd love for you to stop by and check it out when we get back to Clemmington."

"I'd like that," Lena murmured. When she noticed David leaning in and staring at her intently, she took several sips of wine, then changed the subject. "So, I heard from Miles this morning. He confirmed that they'll be arriving in LA this afternoon."

David paused, shifting his body a few inches away from Lena's. "Cool. Who have we got coming from the Clemmington PD again?"

"My dad and brothers, of course. And Officer Underwood. My father asked Russ to stay back and hold down the fort while they're all here."

"Good," David said. "I could use a break from him and his antics."

"You just don't want him flirting with me."

"Yeah, that, too."

Lena's head swiveled as she gazed over at him. "Whoa, okay then. Tell me how you really feel."

David shrugged his shoulders. "Just being honest," he replied before sipping casually from his glass.

"Alrighty then." Lena quickly reopened her laptop and pulled up a Word document. "Listen, why don't we shift gears and run through our plan for catching the killer one more time?"

"Good idea."

"Okay, so, tomorrow night, I'm going to head to the Cucamonga Wilderness hiking trail and revisit the crime scene. Chief Scott has confirmed that he'll have a substantial number of law enforcement officers hidden all along the trail, from the parking lot to the actual crime scene."

"I think I should be posted at the crime scene," David said. "But I'll let you decide where you'd like for me to be positioned."

"Of course I want you posted at the crime scene. That's where the killer will probably try and strike. And when he does, I want you to be there to protect me. Aside from my family, I know that you'll have my back like no one else."

David reached over and took Lena's hand in his.

"Yes, I will," he affirmed.

She leaned back and rested her head on his shoulder.

"Thank you, David."

"Of course." He reached back and slowly wrapped his arm around her. "I know you're probably tired of being questioned, but are you sure you want to do this?"

"Absolutely," Lena said firmly, sitting straight up and refocusing on her computer screen.

Just as she began scrolling down the page, David leaned over and closed her laptop.

"Hey, why don't we give the whole sting operation talk a rest?" he suggested. "We put the plan together back in Clemmington, perfected it over the past few days, shared it with law enforcement and discussed it the whole way here. Believe me. We're good. Let's just take this time to relax. Maybe order some Thai food and chill out until your family gets here."

Lena sat back and let out a deep sigh.

"That actually sounds good. Really good. I'll pull

up Uber Eats and see who can get some food here the fastest. Why don't you scroll through Netflix and find a movie for us to watch?"

"I'd love to."

While David grabbed the remote and turned on the television, Lena curled up on the couch and began searching through restaurants on her phone.

LENA PRESSED HER fingernails into the steering wheel as she sped down Wilson Avenue. She glanced in her rearview mirror for the hundredth time. There, a couple of cars behind her, was the black sedan that Officer Underwood had rented.

She jumped when the shrill sound of her ringing cell phone blasted through the speakers. David's name appeared on the touch screen. She reached out and tapped the accept button.

"Hey," she answered nervously. "What's going on?"

"Just checking in to see how close you are to the hiking trail."

"I'm on Mount Baldy Road now, heading toward Ice House Canyon Road. So I'm about ten minutes away."

"Okay. Your family and I are here at the crime scene, scattered about inconspicuously. And the LAPD is everywhere, posing as joggers, hikers and even a few vagrants."

"Good," Lena breathed, the relief in her voice apparent. "Chief Scott told me he's got several snipers combing the area, too."

"Oh, yeah. We've got this place surrounded. There's

no way in hell the killer is going to find his way out of this trap."

Lena felt her tensed back relax farther into the seat. "Hearing that is definitely helping to calm my nerves. But I have to admit, I'm a bit on edge."

"That's to be expected. And that's why I called you. I wanted to make sure you're holding up okay."

"I am. I just hope that after tonight, this will all be over. I'm tired of living in fear—looking over my shoulder and waiting for the next attack. I'm shaken up right now at the thought that the killer might be following me."

"I know you are. Just stay strong. After tonight, you'll be everybody's hero."

"That is if I get through tonight."

She heard David grunt softly.

"Come on, now," he said. "Don't talk like that. Of course you'll get through tonight. Remember, this go-round, you won't be at the crime scene alone. You'll be surrounded by people who love you, who'd never let anything happen to you."

The sound of those words caused Lena's breath to catch in her throat. She wondered if he was including himself in that group of people who loved her.

"CAN YOU STILL see Officer Underwood in your rear-view?" David asked.

"I can," Lena confirmed after taking a quick look behind her. "I've been keeping an eye out for that obnoxious sports car I think the suspect drives, too. But so far I haven't seen it."

"Well, if he was driving that vehicle all through Clemmington, maybe he was smart enough to switch out cars tonight."

"Maybe…" Lena looked up at the street sign and made a right turn. The sight of vast, rugged mountains came into view. "Okay, I'm heading down Ice House Canyon Road now. So I'll be pulling into the parking lot soon."

"Got it. Once you park your car, just stick to the plan. Let Officer Underwood exit his vehicle first. When he gives you the hand signal that he's got eyes on you, you'll get out of your car and set off toward the trail's entrance."

"Will do. I just need to keep reminding myself that I've got a ton of eyes on me. As vulnerable as I feel right now, I know that I'm safe."

She wasn't quite convinced of her own words. Nevertheless, Lena hoped that saying them out loud would assure her.

"Yes, you are safe," David reiterated. "Now, don't forget to insert your headset before you leave the car. We're all connected through the same network so that we can easily communicate with one another. Anything you see or hear that seems off, let us know. We'll do the same."

"Okay. I'm pulling into the parking lot now. And Officer Underwood is behind me."

"Great. He already has his earpiece in and is keeping us posted on your locations."

Deep breath in, deep breath out… Lena told herself as she parked her car.

The sun had set, and a dark haze covered the canyon. The parking lot had cleared out, and there weren't many vehicles scattered throughout.

Lena turned off her engine and pulled her earpiece out of her purse. She kept her eyes focused on the rearview mirror, waiting for Officer Underwood to make a move.

"Underwood just informed us that he's parked a few spaces away from your car," David said. "He's getting out and heading toward you. Do you see him?"

"I do. He's walking up now. And…he's tapping the screen on his watch. That's my signal. I'm going to disconnect our call, connect my headset and head up the trail to the crime scene."

"Copy that. I'll let the other officers know that you're on the move. Don't forget your forensic kit. We want the suspect to think you're pulling another rogue move and investigating the scene alone."

"I've got it right here on the passenger seat. I'll check back in once I get my headset connected."

"Sounds good. And hey, Lena?"

"Yes?"

"Be careful."

She bit down on the side of her cheek, willing herself to stay calm. Despite being surrounded by law enforcement, she couldn't shake the trembling fear burning inside her stomach.

"I will," Lena said, hoping that David hadn't noticed the crack in her voice.

She ended the call, slipped her Bluetooth headset

inside her ears and tapped the wireless button on her radio adapter.

"Testing, testing, one two," she said. "Can anyone hear me?"

"Coming in clear," Chief Scott replied. "We're all standing by, Lena. I've got officers inconspicuously placed everywhere. You're in good hands."

"Yes, you are," her father added. "I'm positioned at the crime scene with your brothers and David, ready and waiting to move in on the suspect."

"Thanks, everybody. I literally felt my blood pressure easing up with every word you all just spoke."

Lena grabbed her forensic kit and then slowly stepped out of the car. Officer Underwood was several feet ahead, standing along the side of a fence while stretching his calf muscles.

"I'm getting out of the car now," she informed the team.

"We've got eyes on you," Chief Scott replied. "Whenever you're ready, start heading up the trail."

Lena bent down and tightened the laces on her sneakers. She readjusted the waistband on her yellow leggings, then zipped up her white windbreaker.

The colors were much brighter than her normal attire. But Chief Scott had advised her to wear highly visible shades so that she could be easily spotted.

She readjusted the scrunchie holding her ponytail in place and stared up ahead, wondering if the killer was watching her.

"Okay, everyone," Lena said, discreetly moving her

lips. "I'm walking through the parking lot and heading toward the trail's entrance."

"Ten-four," Officer Underwood responded. "I'll be right behind you."

Trembling nerves of doubt crept through her limbs. Her eyes darted from right to left in search of the suspect. She couldn't help but feel as though he would appear out of nowhere and tackle her to the ground.

Stay calm, she told herself. *You are not alone. You're being protected...*

Lena sped up. A blustery wind whipped past her, piercing the tips of her ears. The temperature had dropped significantly since she'd left home. She pulled her zipper all the way up to her chin. But as her teeth began to chatter, she realized that it wasn't just the cool air chilling her to the bone. It was fear.

Deep breath in. Deep breath out.

The breathing mantra failed to ease her nerves. Lena turned her head slightly, hoping to get a glimpse of Officer Underwood walking behind her. But when she didn't see him, a sick feeling of dread spread throughout her entire body.

"I'm still with you, Lena," Officer Underwood said.

The sound of his voice speaking through her earpiece immediately put her at ease.

"We're all watching you," he continued. "Just keep moving forward and act natural. We'll handle the rest."

"Thanks for the reassurance," she responded, covering her mouth as she walked. "You must've sensed that I needed it."

"That, plus the fact that I noticed your head swiveling. I figured you were looking for me."

"You figured correctly," Lena said just as she reached the hiking trail's entrance. "Okay, I'm going in. Did anyone notice whether or not I'm being followed?"

"There is no one in our vicinity," Officer Underwood replied.

Several of the other officers chimed in, confirming that they too hadn't seen anybody.

"Good," she told them. "If that changes, please give me a heads-up."

Lena pulled her flashlight from her jacket pocket and shined the beam on the trail ahead. Just as she began maneuvering her way through the rocks and twigs littering the dried dirt, a throbbing pain pulsated over her right eye.

She grabbed her head, praying that a migraine wasn't about to kick in. Flashes of light and blind spots suddenly clouded her vision. She blinked rapidly, wishing she'd taken a couple of aspirin before leaving home.

It's just stress, she told herself. *Shake it off...*

Lena rubbed her eyes and focused on the trail. The crime scene appeared in the far distance. She stopped, contemplating whether she could finish the mission.

Come on. You can do this...

"You okay up there?" Officer Underwood asked her.

"Yes," she said, lying, her shrill tone laced with forced enthusiasm. "Just stopping for a second to catch my breath."

"Keep going, Lena," she heard David say. "I can see you coming up the trail. You're good."

Hearing his voice was all it took for Lena to move forward. Her slow walk turned into a slight jog. She felt ready to hit the crime scene and get this over with.

Yellow tape came into view. It was about twenty feet off the trail where the victim's body had been found.

Lena slowed down. Her courage began to dwindle again. She second-guessed her decision to do this. Their suspect was slick. She didn't trust that he wouldn't somehow manage to attack her, despite being surrounded by law enforcement.

But it was too late to turn back now. So Lena squared her shoulders and continued into the wooded area.

She eyed the bush that the perp had hidden behind before attacking her the first time. Lena shuffled toward it. She flashed her light toward the shrubbery and bent down, eyeing the area closely. Nothing appeared but dirt and fallen leaves.

Why am I expecting to see the two black lumps that turned out to be the killer's boots? she asked herself.

"You're doing great, Lena," Chief Love said. "Just keep walking the perimeter of the scene. If our perp is here, my guess is that he'll be making an appearance shortly."

No sooner had the words left his mouth than a forceful gust of whistling wind blew past Lena. The hood on her windbreaker flew across her face, blocking her vision. The sound of rustling foliage and crackling branches filled the air. It was as if the entire forest had burst into song, playing a haunting melody.

Lena felt herself becoming unnerved. She dropped her forensic kit and pulled her hood away from her face. Flashbacks of the attack flooded her mind. She spun around, searching for the killer. She could sense his presence. Lena knew he was going to attack at any given moment.

The spinning caused her to grow dizzy. The stress wasn't helping. Lena stopped, feeling as though she might pass out.

"Lena!" she heard David say. "Are you okay? Do you need assistance?"

His voice once again calmed her heightened sense of panic. She closed her eyes and took a deep breath in, then out.

"I'm fine," she said. "I just—I've got a headache. It made me feel a little discombobulated. But I'm good."

Lena picked up her forensic kit and kept going. There was no way in hell she could let the entire LAPD down, let alone the Clemmington PD. This case was riding on her, and she was determined to see it through.

The rustling of the tree branches ceased. The eerie wind subsided. A strange sense of peace lingered in the air.

See? Lena said to herself. *Everything's okay. Just stay the course.*

And then…

Boom!

Lena hit the ground. She was pinned against the dirt. What felt like a two-hundred-pound mass was lying on top of her. She tried to scream, but her face was being pressed against the chalky earth.

Suddenly, the weight was lifted off her. She was flipped over onto her back, then pulled to her feet.

A bewildered Lena rubbed the dirt from her eyes and stared straight ahead. She struggled to comprehend what had just happened.

"Freeze!" she heard her father and Chief Scott yelling simultaneously.

A swarm of law enforcement officers were huddled together, hovering over someone.

"Hands above your head! Let me see your hands!" the group roared.

Lena felt someone run up from behind and spin her around. It was David.

"Are you all right?" he asked her. "He didn't hurt you, did he? I'm so sorry we didn't get to you sooner."

Lena embraced him tightly, laying her head against his chest as she tried to catch her breath.

"What—what *happened*?" she stammered.

"The killer just jumped out of a tree and took you down," David replied, wrapping his arms around her protectively. "I'm so glad we were able to get to him before he could harm you. And you did great. Thanks to you, we got him."

"Thank God," Lena whispered, still shaken up but relieved that everything was finally over.

David held on to her as he headed toward the trail.

"Come on," he said. "Let's get you out of here."

Chapter Seventeen

David leaned back in his seat and stared across the table, looking into the eyes of their suspect.

They were sitting inside a small LAPD interrogation room. Bleak gray walls matched the worn carpet. The black plastic chairs were uncomfortable, and the steel metal table was cold. David felt claustrophobic being stuffed between Chief Love and Chief Scott. But he wasn't there for the creature comforts. He was there to get a confession.

David glanced discreetly over at the reflective glass window. He couldn't see through it. But he knew that Lena, her brothers and several other law enforcement officers were standing on the other side, looking on from the observation room.

"How old did you say you were again?" David asked the perp.

"I didn't," he replied defiantly.

"Hmm." David sighed. He ran his hand down his goatee, studying the suspect.

The man appeared to be about five feet eleven inches tall. He had a stocky build and was dressed in tactical camouflage gear. His look fit Lena's description of her attacker to a T.

"Listen," David continued, "I would advise you to drop the whole tough-guy act. You're currently in police custody, being questioned by two police chiefs and a detective regarding some of the most heinous crimes that the state of California has ever seen. Do you understand that?"

"Um, *no*," the suspect shot back, fiddling with the handcuffs clinging to his wrists. "I'm telling you, you've got the wrong guy. Now can one of you please get me outta these shackles? It's not like I committed a real crime or anything."

"Attacking a woman out on a hiking trail *is* a real crime," David shot back. "Not to mention the rest of the felonies we're questioning you about. So we'll remove the cuffs after we get some answers."

David noticed a sudden change in the suspect's disposition. No longer was his head held high and chest poked out. He was now hunched over, his gaze focused on the table rather than the law enforcement officers.

"Son," Chief Scott began, "why don't you start by telling us your real name."

After several moments of silence, the suspect finally spoke up. "Chris."

"Chris *what*?" Chief Love asked.

"Chris Ware."

"As in Christopher Ware?"

"Yeah."

"And how old are you?" David asked once again while jotting down notes.

"Eighteen."

The detective and police chiefs glanced at one another, their furrowed brows a clear indication that they were all on the same page. None of them expected their perp to be so young.

"Look," Christopher said, "I don't know what type of…*hernias* crimes you all think I committed. But whatever they are, I didn't do 'em."

David shook his head in disgust. He didn't know whether to correct or slap him. He decided to do neither and instead continued his line of questioning.

"What were you doing hanging out in the middle of the Cucamonga Wilderness trail? In the middle of a blocked-off crime scene, no less?"

Christopher glared at David, remaining silent. The detective prayed that he wouldn't cut the interview short and ask for an attorney.

"That's what I was instructed to do," Christopher finally blurted out.

"What do you mean, *instructed to do*?" Chief Scott asked.

The suspect shoved his right hand inside his mouth and began biting down on his grubby fingernails. David slid his chair closer to the perp and leaned in, sensing that he was about to break.

"Who instructed you to go out on that trail?" he asked quietly, hoping that the softer tone would encourage him to talk.

Christopher's knees bounced erratically underneath the table. He swiped his hand across his perspiring forehead.

"Come on, Chris," David urged. "You need to tell us what's really going on here. I'd hate to arrest and charge you with multiple counts of first degree murder if you weren't involved in the crimes."

"First degree murder!" Christopher shouted. He shifted in his seat and began rocking back and forth. "Wait, this interrogation isn't a part of the prank?"

"Prank?" Chief Love spat. "What prank?"

"Ugh," Christopher moaned, dropping his head into his hands. "I got set up, man…"

"By whom?" David asked, throwing his arms out from his sides. "Listen. It's been a long, nerve-racking day. We're all exhausted. You need to stop speaking in fragments and tell us what the hell is going on here."

Christopher looked back up at the officers, his red eyes appearing damp. "I'll probably get arrested for what I'm about to tell you. But at least I won't get charged with murder. So, here goes."

When he paused, Chief Scott slid his tape recorder across the table and turned up the volume. "We're listening."

Christopher looked up at the white ceiling tiles and blinked rapidly. "There's this shock site on the dark web called *Gonna Get Got*. The guys who run it post violent videos, extreme prank videos, stuff like that."

He paused once again. David tapped his pen against the table, his skin prickling with irritation as Christopher took several long sips of soda.

Be patient, he told himself. *At least you've got him talking…*

David winced when their perp emitted a loud burp.

"And," Christopher continued, "there's a section on the site that lets members apply for prank master positions. That's what I am. So when *Gonna Get Got* receives requests to have pranks pulled on someone, we're hired to do the job. I've been taking on jobs since last year. This was my eighth assignment. And I have never, *ever* been busted by the cops before. Until now, that is."

"Okay," David replied, staring down at the table while struggling to digest the absurd story. "What exactly did this particular assignment entail?"

"First, I had to send in a photo of myself to prove that I fit the description of the job requirements."

"And what was that description?"

"Male, about five feet eleven inches tall, husky build. Oh, and I had to buy this outfit I'm wearing and send in a photo of it before I got hired."

David paused. He eyed Christopher from head to toe. A cold sweat seeped through his pores once he realized that the real suspect had hired a stunt double to foil their sting operation.

"How exactly do you communicate with these people?" David asked. "Is it strictly through the website?"

"Yeah. *Gonna Get Got* lets its members chat back and forth without revealing their identities."

"So you have no idea who these people are that you're working with?"

"Nope. And as long as I'm getting paid, I honestly don't care."

When David groaned loudly and leaned back in his chair, Chief Scott stepped in.

"Well, you *should* care," he insisted. "Because you're dealing with some really dangerous people here. Now explain to us what you were instructed to do tonight."

"Look, the dude sent me a photo of some woman who he said was an old childhood friend, and a map of the Cucamonga Wilderness hiking trail. I was told to camp out at the taped-off spot last night and wait for the woman in the picture to show up today. When she did, the plan was for me to jump her, knock her to the ground, then yell *gotcha!*"

"Gotcha?" David asked. "Why gotcha?"

"Because that's the site's catchphrase or whatever." David slid toward the edge of his chair.

"So let me get this straight," he began. "You were there at the site when law enforcement officers arrived earlier this afternoon?"

"Yep. And when I saw you all coming, I hid in a tree. I didn't know what role you all were playing in the prank. So I got out of Dodge and stuck to the script. I wasn't about to miss out on making five hundred dollars."

"Five hundred dollars," Chief Love repeated, as if shocked at the amount.

Christopher nodded his head arrogantly. "Yes, sirs."

"Wait," David said, holding up his hand. "Do you still have the picture of the woman that was sent to you?"

"I think so. It's on my cell phone. In my jacket pocket."

David glanced over at the chiefs. They both nodded their heads, indicating it was okay to uncuff him.

David stood up and unlocked Christopher's restraints. The suspect pulled out his phone, tapped the screen, then handed it to him.

"Here she is."

David leaned forward. His stomach flipped at the sight of Lena's image splayed across the screen. He immediately recognized where the photo had come from. It was her profile picture on Instagram.

Both of the chiefs moved in closer and eyed the photo. David could feel the anger coming off them as they grunted simultaneously, then looked away.

David turned his attention back to Christopher, anxious to pump him for more information.

"Did the person requesting this job share with you the reason behind wanting to have this woman attacked?" he asked.

"Yep," Christopher said before taking several more sips of soda.

David felt a sudden urge to jump across the table and strangle him.

"*Well*, what was it?" he prompted.

"He said that him and the woman had been pulling pranks on each other for years. A few weeks ago, they were jogging out on that trail, and she faked like she was having a heart attack. The guy thought she was dead. Scared the crap outta him. So he wanted to get back at her. He knew she'd be out there running today and sent me to prank her."

Chief Love slammed his fist against the table and jumped up from his chair.

"Looks like the only ones who got *got* is us!" he

barked, before walking out and slamming the door behind him.

David could tell by the distressed frown on Chief Scott's face that he wanted to follow suit. But David wasn't ready to let up.

"So, how do you receive your payments?" he continued.

"Anonymously. Through a mobile payment service."

David closed his eyes and rubbed them rigorously. Chief Love was right. The only ones who'd been had was them.

"So, uh," Christopher began, "am I gonna get arrested? Or can I get sent home for good behavior?"

Chief Scott tapped David's arm and stood up.

"Why don't we take a break?" he suggested.

"I think that's a good idea," David told him. "Christopher, give us a minute. We'll be back soon."

"Yeah, sure. I mean…um—sirs, yes, sirs!" he hollered, jumping up from his chair and saluting them as they left the room.

"Just keep walking," the chief muttered to David.

"Hey!" Christopher called out. "When you corporals come back, can you bring me another soda? And maybe a corned beef sandwich with a bag of chips or something—"

David shut the door behind him before Christopher could finish.

"I cannot believe this…this *foolery*!" Chief Scott roared. "How am I supposed to go inside that observation room and face Lena? We really screwed this up, Detective."

"Chief, we're pulling out all the stops to try and solve this case. Lena knows that. Every plan isn't going to work, unfortunately. But hopefully we're getting closer. And keep in mind we are dealing with a cold, calculated, highly intelligent psychopath here. Organized serial killers like this one are the most difficult to catch."

Chief Scott leaned against the wall. He pulled a handkerchief from his shirt pocket and ran it across his sweaty, balding head. "You're right. But in hindsight, putting out that fake press release was a bad idea. The killer guessed right. He figured out what we were doing and used it against us. Imagine how thrilled he must be right now."

"Yeah, well, it was still a good effort," David insisted, giving the chief's arm a supportive pat. "And if the suspect is in fact gloating, then he'd better enjoy his freedom while it lasts. Because now that he's pissed off your entire force *and* Clemmington's? Trust me. This will be the last time he gets one over on us."

"Let's hope so. We have *got* to get this maniac off the street before he strikes again."

"We will." David glanced over at the observation room door. "Should we go in and check on our girl?"

"Yes. We should. Then we'll regroup and figure out what to do with that goofball *prank master* Christopher."

David stifled a chuckle and followed Chief Scott inside the room. He noticed Lena's father embracing her tightly.

Chief Scott paused. He glanced over at a group of LAPD officers huddled in a corner.

"Could you all please give us a minute?" he asked them. "I'd like to have a word with Lena and the Clemmington PD."

"Yes, sir," the officers said as they walked out.

Once the door was closed, Chief Scott approached Lena.

"I cannot apologize to you enough for what happened tonight," he began. "We put everything we had into this operation. However, I had no idea that our suspect would figure out—"

Lena's father held up his hand.

"I'm sorry to interrupt you, Chief. But that's not why Lena's upset. She just received a very disturbing email."

Miles handed Lena's phone to Chief Scott. David peered over his shoulder, eyeing the message.

My Dearest Lena,
You poor, pitiful soul. Did you and your little comrades really think I would be stupid enough to fall for that amateur trap? Yes? Well LOL, the joke's on you, bitch! The LAPD must really be disappointed in you. Do you think they'll miss you when you're dead? Because for my next act, I won't be pulling a prank. I'll be carving the other half of that heart into your chest, then choking the life out of you. Enjoy your last days while you can...
Yours truly,
Committer of the Heart-Shaped Murders

David's entire body shook with rage. He looked over at Lena, devastated by the sight of her tearstained face.

"Your computer forensics expert is already investigating the origins of the email," Miles told Chief Scott. "He's assuming that the killer sent the message using a VPN that would hide his identity. But he's going to take a crack at it anyway."

"Good," David said, hoping that no one noticed the tremor in his tone. "The Clemmington PD already looked into another email Lena received from him. It was sent through an encrypted VPN tunnel. And the text messages she's been getting were delivered through a secure app that doesn't store data. So we were unable to trace them back to the sender."

"My God." Chief Scott sighed before handing the phone back to Miles. "Who in the hell are we dealing with here?"

"Have you thought about bringing in the FBI?" Jake asked the chief.

"I have. But I'm hesitant. We've made a lot of headway on this case. I don't want them coming in and trying to take over."

"At this point, maybe we should consider it," Chief Love interjected. "I know we're highly skilled and all, but I think it's safe to say we might be in over our heads with this one."

"What do you think, Lena?" David asked her softly. "Should we continue this investigation on our own? Or is it time to bring in reinforcements?"

She opened her mouth to speak. But instead of a response, Lena shrugged her shoulders.

"David," her father said, "why don't you take Lena home? We'll stay here and wrap things up with Christopher." He glanced down at his daughter. "Are you okay with that, hon?"

She stepped away from him and nodded her head, still unable to speak.

"And you're sure you don't need to go to the hospital and get checked out?"

"No," she said. "I'm fine. I just wanna get out of here."

David walked over and wrapped his arm around her protectively. "Come on. Let's get you home."

Miles gave Lena a quick hug and patted David on the back. "We'll call and check in with you all once we get back to the hotel."

"Sounds good, man," David replied. "Thanks."

"See you soon, sis," Jake said.

Lena threw him a feeble wave, then leaned into David as he held on to her tightly. The pair walked through the station in silence. Just when they reached the exit, she stopped abruptly and turned to him.

"I don't think I can do this anymore," she blurted out. "Maybe we do need to bring in the FBI. And— and I should stop working the case. As a matter of fact, maybe I need to stop working as a forensic investigator altogether. Because at this point, these murders are happening because of me. It's *my* fault these people are being killed."

"Hold on, Lena. Listen to me. You are not the cause of these murders. So don't put that on yourself. Now, you're exhausted and shaken up, which is perfectly understandable. Let's not make any rash decisions. Why don't we go back to your place, order some food and get some rest? Drop all talk of the investigation for now. How does that sound?"

Lena stared up at David. The expression on her face was so soft and vulnerable that he almost bent down and kissed her.

"That sounds good," she whispered before allowing him to lead her out the door.

Chapter Eighteen

"This might sound weird," Lena said, "but I am so happy to be back in Clemmington."

"That does sound weird, coming from you," her mother agreed, reaching across the kitchen table and clutching her daughter's hand. "I'm glad to hear it, though. But once again, I wish your visit was under more pleasant circumstances."

"Yeah. So do I."

It had been three days since Lena left LA. She tried to hang in there and continue assisting with the investigation. But she'd grown frustrated when Christopher was only charged with minor assault and released from the county jail due to overcrowding. He also hadn't provided law enforcement with any information that would help lead them to the killer.

Then when the LAPD failed to make any headway or come up with a new plan to catch the suspect, she decided that she'd had enough. Lena and David packed up and headed back to Clemmington, rejoining her father and brothers, who'd left the city two days after the botched sting operation.

"I just feel more comfortable being here at home, surrounded by my family," Lena said.

"As you should. There's nothing like family, honey. No matter the situation, you can always depend on us. And I'm including David in that equation, too."

"So am I," Lena responded, giving her mother's hand a slight squeeze.

"Speaking of David, what's going on between you two?"

"What do you mean?"

Betty threw Lena a sly side-eye. "You know what I mean."

"No, actually I don't," Lena insisted, playing coy before jumping up from the table and grabbing their coffee cups. "Time for a couple of refills. Do you want another muffin?"

Her mother chuckled and waved Lena off. "Way to change the conversation, kiddo. You always were good at that."

"Good at what?" she shot back, continuing to deflect from the topic at hand. "Look, all I'm saying is that I'd like to splurge on another chocolate chip muffin. Will you be joining me?"

"Twist my arm, why don't you. Meaning yes, throw a chocolate croissant on a plate for me."

Lena refilled their cups with hazelnut coffee and set them on a tray, added the plate of pastries, and carried it over to the table.

"Can you at least admit that you and David share a special bond?" Betty asked.

Lena sighed as she sat back down. "Yes, I can admit

that David and I share a special bond. But as far as us getting back together is concerned, I don't see that happening."

"Why not?"

"Because our past is so rocky. And I can't help but think that a part of him still resents me for moving away. He believes that's what ultimately ruined our relationship."

"Did he tell you that?" Betty asked.

"In so many words, yes."

Her mother sat quietly, taking several sips of coffee before turning to her daughter.

"A lot's changed since then, Lena. I personally think you and David are good for one another. And with you spending so much time here in town, working down at the station with him and your dad and brothers, it seems to me that everything is falling into place."

"Yeah, except the fact that this serial killer is still on the loose. Honestly, Mom? Until he's been apprehended, I can't even think about anything else."

"I can understand that. I'm sorry, honey. I'll drop it. But I do have something else on my mind. Now that you're back home, please don't run off on your own and investigate any more crime scenes. I don't care what happens. Understood?"

Lena stared down at her muffin and picked at the chocolate chips.

"Understood," she muttered.

The conversation was interrupted when Lena's cell phone buzzed. Her mother stood up and grabbed her coffee and croissant.

"I'll let you get that while I head to my bedroom," Betty said. "My book club's Zoom meeting is starting in a few minutes."

"Okay. Enjoy."

Lena grabbed her cell. The words *No Caller ID* appeared on the screen.

She held her hand to her chest. Her heartbeat stuttered erratically as she debated whether or not to answer the call.

The old you would've picked up on the first ring, she thought to herself.

But things had changed. Ever since the brutal attack, she no longer possessed that fiery sense of fearlessness.

The call went to voice mail. Lena studied the screen, waiting to see if the caller would leave a message.

She jumped back in her seat when the phone buzzed again. The person was calling back.

"Come on, you can do this," Lena said out loud. "Answer the call."

On the fourth ring, she finally got up the nerve to pick up. "Hello?"

"Hel-hello. May I, uh…may I please speak to Lena Love?"

Lena sat back in her seat, confused at the sound of the woman's soft, timid voice.

"Speaking," she said. "May I ask who's calling?"

"Um, I'd rather not say."

"Okay," Lena replied slowly. "How may I help you?"

The caller remained silent.

Lena stood up and walked over to the deck's sliding glass doors. She stared out into the backyard, contemplating whether she should hang up the phone. But something told her to stay on the line.

"Hello?" Lena asked. "Are you still there?"

"I'm here. I just— I'm a little nervous, that's all. Actually, I'm a lot nervous."

"Why is that?"

"Because I've got some information that may help solve your murder investigation."

Lena jumped back so fast that she almost tumbled to the floor. She grabbed hold of the door handle and slid it open, then stepped out onto the deck. Her bare feet pounded against the cedar boards as she began pacing back and forth.

"I'm listening," Lena said, biting her tongue so she wouldn't bombard the woman with a barrage of questions.

"So, the killer. I think you know him."

Lena stopped abruptly. It felt as though a splinter had torn through her heel. But she was too focused on the conversation to acknowledge the pain.

"Really?" she panted. "And what would make you think that?"

"I can't tell you. Just trust me. You do."

Lena looked out at the alleyway in the back of the house, just to make sure that the squad car was still there. It was. Ever since she'd returned to Clemmington, her father had cruisers patrolling both the front and back of the house at all times.

"Well," Lena said, "are you going to tell me who you think the killer is?"

"I want to. But I can't."

"Look, is this some type of prank call? Because I honestly don't have time to—"

"This is *not* a prank call," the woman interrupted. "I'm trying to clue you in on who I think the killer is without saying too much. If I do, I'd never forgive myself."

Lena walked over to the edge of the deck and leaned against the railing.

"Why is that?" she asked.

"Because I know the person. All too well."

"Okay then." Lena sighed. "What *can* you tell me?"

The other end of the line went silent for several seconds.

"Hello?" Lena practically shouted.

"I'm here. Sorry. Like I said, I'm nervous."

Lena closed her eyes and inhaled slowly.

Be patient, she told herself. *Let the woman go at her own pace.*

The sound of heavy panting came swooshing through Lena's eardrum.

"Your suspect runs a website called *Gonna Get Got*," the caller blurted out.

Lena's eyes shot open. She gripped the phone after it almost slipped out of her hand.

This call is legit...

"Wait," Lena said. "How do you know that?"

"Like I said, I don't feel comfortable sharing too much information. For a number of reasons. There's too much at stake. Just take what I'm giving you and go from there. Find the person who runs the site, and you'll find your killer."

"Listen, you have *got* to help me out here. Please. I'm begging you."

The other end of the phone went silent once again.

"Please," Lena insisted as tears filled her eyes. "I'm desperate. And I—"

"I saw the video of you being attacked out on the hiking trail on the *Gonna Get Got* website," the woman interrupted.

"What? How? Who recorded it? The LAPD caught the kid who attacked me. He didn't do it. Law enforcement ran an analysis on his phone."

"Your suspect recorded it."

Lena froze. Despite the steamy California heat, she was overcome by a frigid chill. The thought of the killer being at the scene, filming the prank while surrounded by two police forces, almost brought her to her knees.

"Are you still there?" the woman asked.

"Yes. I'm here. I, uh—I'm in shock over what you just told me."

"I can imagine." The caller paused, then inhaled sharply. "Look, I will tell you this. When it comes to *Gonna Get Got*, your suspect usually hires what he calls prank masters to do the jobs. But if a request comes in one thousand dollars or more, he'll perform the prank himself."

"One thousand dollars," Lena blurted out. "What kind of prank is worth that much money?"

"The deadly kind."

"Wait. People are paying this man to commit murder?"

"Not exactly. They're paying him to bring people to the brink of death. Just to mess with their heads."

Lena's mind raced as she began pacing the deck again. A flurry of questions flew through her head. She ran back inside the house and into the dining room.

"And another thing I noticed," the woman continued, "is that your suspect seems to take on jobs that'll give him some sort of personal satisfaction—"

She abruptly stopped speaking. Lena heard the sound of a man's voice booming in the background.

"Jan!" he yelled. "You home?"

"I've gotta go!" the woman hissed.

"Wait! Can you just finish what you were saying? What do you mean by *personal satisfaction*?"

"You're gonna have to figure that out for yourself."

Lena flung open her laptop. "Well, can you at least tell me how to gain access to the website—"

Before she could finish, the line went dead.

"Dammit!" Lena yelled.

Her fingers fumbled as she tried to dial David's cell phone number. On the third attempt, she finally succeeded. But the call went straight to voice mail.

"David! Call me ASAP! I just received some new information about the case."

Lena disconnected the call and frantically typed a text message to him, insisting that he call her immediately.

After sending the message, she thought about her

car. She was so tempted to jump inside, rush down to the police station and find David.

Don't do it, a voice inside her head warned. *You made a promise to your family. And to David...*

Lena slammed her laptop shut. A fiery ball of anger exploded inside her chest. She couldn't stand the hold that this killer had on her. It'd left her feeling anxious and powerless.

You have got to think of something. Something that'll catch him at his own game...

Chapter Nineteen

David slid his laptop toward Lena and enlarged the website displayed on the screen.

"My digital forensic investigator was able to download a dark web browser onto my laptop, which enabled access to *Gonna Get Got*," he said. "Our search capabilities are limited, though. We won't be able to view any of the videos or other exclusive content until our membership is approved. Once it is, we can go from there."

Lena leaned forward, focusing on the computer screen while sipping a glass of wine. "Wonderful. I'm just glad we were able to gain access."

She and David were sitting in the middle of his living room, cozied up on his chocolate-brown leather sofa. After receiving Lena's messages earlier that day about the anonymous phone call, David immediately went to work on infiltrating the website.

"It looks pretty sinister, doesn't it?" David asked, pointing at the screen. "That black background against the eerie, bright red font."

"A font that appears to be bleeding, no less."

"Exactly. And the logo, with the GGG lettering and photo of a distorted Japanese oni mask, is quite disturbing. Those three *G*'s actually remind me of the devil's number, 666."

"Well, think about it," Lena said. "An oni is an evil being that haunts the spirit world. Our killer is an evil man who's haunting the entire state of California. Seems fitting to me."

"Yes, it does."

Goose bumps formed underneath the raised hairs on David's forearms as he studied the oni's image. Two large gold horns were growing from its head. Its long, wild hair, cracked red skin, and ogre-like features were chilling.

David tapped the menu button. "We need to figure out how to navigate this site. The administrator certainly doesn't make it easy to access any of the content. Even the stuff that isn't exclusive."

"Seems like that's all a part of the allure. Figuring out how to crack the code just adds to the mystery. If this is how our suspect spends his free time, it gives us even more insight into how twisted he really is."

David could feel Lena's eyes on him as he continued to search the site. When she slid closer toward him, her thigh brushed up against his. A bolt of heat shot straight up his leg and settled in his groin.

Stay focused, he told himself while trying not to squirm in his seat. *Tonight is about business. This is not a social call…*

"Thank you again for having me over for dinner," Lena said. "I really needed this."

"And I need for you to stop thanking me. Like I told you earlier, this was the least I could do. You've been working so hard and taking so many hits with this investigation. So for me to throw a couple of mouthwatering steaks and ears of corn on the grill, sauté a little asparagus, and stop off at your favorite bakery to pick up a silky vanilla key lime pie was nothing."

Lena squeezed David's shoulder playfully, then held her hand to her ear. "What was that I just heard? Could it have been the sound of you tooting your own horn?"

He sat straight up and glanced around the room. "Huh? I didn't hear a thing."

Her hand drifted down toward the small of his back. David was surprised when she kept it there.

"I do have to admit, though," she said, "dinner was delicious. You outdid yourself. It certainly was a big change up from all the noodles, chicken nuggets and tater tots you used to cook back in the day."

"Um, excuse me. Let's not get it twisted. If I can recall correctly, you used to devour everything I made."

"Yeah, I did," Lena quipped. She took a sip of wine, then paused.

When David glanced over at her, she smiled slightly. It appeared as though Lena was lost in thought.

"On a serious note," she continued, "there's something else that I'd like to thank you for."

"Really? What's that?"

"Thank you for always taking care of me. And protecting me. And wanting what's best for me. I do realize that I could've handled things better before I moved to LA. But I was so eager to get my career started that

I neglected to deal with our relationship the right way. As well as your feelings. So for that, I apologize."

David parted his lips to speak. But he couldn't find the right words to say. He was too taken aback. Because everything Lena had just said was all he ever wanted to hear.

"And you don't have to respond to any of that," she added. "We can leave it right there. I just wanted you to know how I was feeling."

David cleared his throat. "Well, I appreciate you sharing that with me. It means a lot. More than you'll ever know, actually."

"Now you're making me wish I would've shared it a long time ago."

"You should have. I think it would have avoided a lot of hurt feelings and resentment. At least on my end."

"Mine, too," Lena murmured.

David felt a singeing arousal swirl inside his chest. His eyes searched Lena's remorseful expression and landed on her soft lips. They lingered along the curves of her petite figure, which was well-defined in her fitted white jumpsuit. The sight of her voluptuous cleavage, which was perfectly positioned within the low-cut neckline, caused him to readjust his navy trousers.

"Would you like another glass of wine?" he asked, eager to change the subject in hopes that it would quell his excitement. "Or a second piece of pie?"

Lena placed her hand over her flat stomach. "If I put another morsel of food inside my mouth, I swear my jumper might burst at the seams. So no. I'll pass on the pie. I may have one more glass of wine in a bit, though. But for now, why don't we try and figure out how to find our way around this *Gonna Get Got* site?"

"Good idea. Oh, and didn't you mention earlier that you came up with some sort of plan you think might help us catch the killer?"

Lena twisted her lips and shrugged her shoulders, as if she were having second thoughts. "Eh, I thought I had something, but I don't know if it'll work."

"Look, at this point we need all the ideas we can get. So come on. Let's hear it."

She stared down at her fidgeting fingers. "After we tried to pull off the whole press release ruse and failed, I don't know how you'd feel about this."

"Try me."

"All right. Here goes. Once we receive the confirmation that we're officially members of the *Gonna Get Got* site, we should submit some sort of high-price prank request that we know the killer will take on himself."

"Hmm." David sighed thoughtfully, running his hand down his goatee. "You know what? I actually like that idea. I like it a lot."

"You do?"

"Yeah. I do. But whatever we come up with has got to be foolproof and go off without a hitch. We can't afford another misstep."

"I agree."

"So what type of prank did you have in mind?"

Lena paused once again. As she stared down at her

glass, David got the sense that she was holding something back.

"I know that expression," he said. "The rapidly blinking eyes. The tightened lips. I still remember it from back in the day, when you'd want to share something with me but were afraid of how I'd react. As a matter of fact, it's the look you gave me right before you announced your move to LA."

Lena sat back and stared at him intently. "Sometimes I hate that you know me so well. Better than anyone else, honestly."

Maybe it's an indication that we belong together, David almost blurted out. But he quickly caught himself.

"So come on then," he continued. "Let's hear the plan."

"Okay, but before I start, promise me that you'll keep an open mind."

"Uh-oh." David picked up the bottle of Pinot Noir and refilled their glasses. "Sounds like this is gonna require more wine."

"Trust me, it will." Lena grabbed her glass and took a long sip before continuing. "So, while I don't have an *exact* plan for the prank request that we should submit, I do have a couple of suggestions. First, I think we should set the price high on how much we're willing to pay. That way, we can guarantee that the killer will take on the job himself."

"Good thinking. And I agree."

"I also think that we should use me as the subject.

Let our suspect know in advance that the prank is aimed directly at me."

David abruptly pushed his laptop off to the side and jumped up from the couch.

"*Absolutely* not," he insisted.

David noticed Lena flinch as he stormed across the mahogany hardwood floor. He stopped at the picture window, staring up at the bright three-quarter moon in search of the right words to say.

Chill, he told himself. *Don't lose your cool and ruin the evening over a bad idea.*

David turned back around.

"I hope you're joking right now," he said. "Because you cannot seriously be making such a reckless suggestion."

Lena set her glass down on the table and stood up. She walked over to David and took his hands in hers.

Her soft, warm touch caused his anger level to drop several notches. David's heaving chest settled as he stared down at her.

"Just hear me out," she said softly. "You're the one who said we can't afford any missteps this go-round. We've got to do something that will guarantee an arrest. Everything we've tried so far hasn't worked. But finding out that this man runs a website that could give us direct access to him is priceless. We have got to seize this opportunity. And unless we come up with a plan that'll put us in his presence, we'll keep failing, and he'll keep killing."

"But what if your plan gets *you* killed?"

"It won't. I trust that Clemmington's police force,

along with the LAPD, will protect me. And honestly, if we don't do something soon, he's going to kill me anyway."

Lena's words chilled David to his core. He remained silent for several moments before giving her hands a gentle squeeze.

"Look," he said, "I can't say that I agree with your idea one hundred percent. But I'm willing to be open-minded while we work on a viable plan."

"That's all I'm asking you to do. Now, why don't we drop the subject for now? Let's sit back down and finish our wine."

David felt the tingling sensation of Lena's thumbs caressing his palms. He stood there for a moment, gazing at her. His mind drifted to the past, back when they were still together and happily in love.

He took a step toward her. She leaned into his chest. Just as he bent down and pressed his lips against hers, his cell phone vibrated inside his pocket.

"Ooh!" Lena gasped, quickly backing away from him.

David couldn't tell which she was more startled by—the kiss or the phone.

"Sorry about that," he muttered, irritated by the interruption.

He reached down and pulled out the phone. A text message from his digital forensic investigator appeared on the screen.

Your membership to the *Gonna Get Got* website has been activated. You'll now be able to create a profile, send and receive messages, and access exclusive content. Let me know if there's anything I can do to assist in the investigation.

"We're in," David said as he wrapped his arm around Lena's waist and led her back over to the couch.

As much as David wanted to cross the line and take their relationship in a more intimate direction, he knew that now was not the time. They needed to stick to the business at hand—catching the killer before he struck again.

Chapter Twenty

Dear *Gonna Get Got* Administrator,
I would like to hire a prank master to pull a stunt on my ex-girlfriend. I want her to think that this is a real-life situation, and I am her hero. My goal is to get her back. Below are the details of the job:

The prank will take place in the city of Berkshire, at a restaurant called The Ocean Grill. I know the owner and will make arrangements for him to rent the place out to me after hours. I'll bring my ex there, giving her the impression that this is a private dinner date and I'm issuing an elaborate apology.

I will drop her off in front of the restaurant while I go and park the car. The prank master will act as the restaurant's maître d' and escort her inside. He'll need to wear a full disguise. Wig, beard, glasses, the whole nine, so that he's unrecognizable. He will take my ex down to the restaurant's lower level. Once the door closes behind them, he'll lock it and pull out a fake gun. He'll then tie her up and hold her hostage, acting as if he's going to rob her.

That's when I'll show up, banging on the door. The

prankster will give her the impression that he's going to kill me. I'll kick the door in and rush down the stairs. The fake gun will shoot blanks. I'll act as if I'm dodging the bullets, and the prank master and I will get into a pseudo tussle. I'll overtake him, grab hold of the gun, and keep him at bay until my ex and I can escape. We will flee the scene and I'll act as if I'm calling the police. I won't. I will have someone call me and pretend that the suspect got away before cops arrived.

I have attached a photo of my ex-girlfriend. I am willing to pay $2,000 for this prank. I hope that you agree to these terms, and look forward to hearing back from you. Thank you.

Lena read over the message one last time, then emailed it to David for his approval.

The pair had worked on the plan for three days straight after their dinner at his house. Once they settled on the specifics, Lena agreed to draft the details.

But the plan laid out in the message wasn't the one they intended to follow. An undercover LAPD officer would play the role of Lena's ex-boyfriend and drive her to the restaurant. The Ocean Grill was owned by a friend of Berkshire's police chief, so he'd be in on the stunt.

The Clemmington PD and LAPD would have The Ocean Grill discreetly surrounded. As soon as the undercover cop pulled in front of the restaurant, Lena would step out of the car. When the killer approached the vehicle to escort her inside, law enforcement would jump in and place him under arrest.

That was the plan. Lena prayed that this time, it would actually work.

Her thoughts were interrupted by a ping from her laptop. She rolled over to the other side of her bed and double-clicked the email inbox. A new message from David popped up on the screen.

Your request to *Gonna Get Got* looks great. I'll send it to Chief Love and Chief Scott for their approval. You know that neither of them are fully on board with this idea. They both think it's radical and dangerous. Nevertheless, since you're set on the plan and we've run out of options, they're willing to go with it. We just have to prove that our strategy to keep you safe is bulletproof. I'll keep you posted on their responses.

Lena wrote David back, letting him know that she'd be anxiously waiting to hear back from him. She then closed out her email and pulled up the internet.

Clemmington PD's digital forensic investigator had downloaded the dark web browser onto her laptop so that she could access *Gonna Get Got*. To say that she'd become obsessed with the site was an understatement. Lena had viewed practically every video that'd been posted, from the funnier pranks to the more intense, to those that were downright dark and evil.

For some reason, she hadn't been able to find the video of Christopher attacking her out on the Cucamonga hiking trail. She wondered if the killer had taken it down.

She refreshed the website one last time. Lena suspected that a new video had not been posted within the last few minutes. But she couldn't help but check anyway.

Just as she placed her hand along the top of the laptop to shut it, a huge ball of fire burst onto the screen. The sound of a detonating bomb blasted through the speakers. The words *NEW VIDEO ALERT!!!* flashed rapidly.

Lena shot straight up and pulled her computer in closer.

"What the…"

She leaned forward and double-clicked the play button. The screen faded to black. The word *DISLOYALTY* slowly appeared. Its bold red letters grew larger as they moved to the forefront. The haunting beat of an ominous bass drum boomed in the background.

Lena held her breath. The screen faded to black again. Then a brightly lit kitchen appeared. A woman was standing at a stainless steel sink, staring out the window. Her back was to the camera. She was holding a cell phone up to her ear.

The sound of the bass drum abruptly stopped.

"You're gonna have to figure that out for yourself," the woman whispered into the phone.

She disconnected the call and turned around. The white scrunchie holding her long blond hair in place fell to the floor. Her pale green eyes widened. Her body stiffened at the sight of whoever was holding the camera.

"What are you doing?" Lena heard the man holding the camera ask.

"Nothing," the woman croaked. "I was—I was just, uh, washing up a few dishes."

The cameraman crept toward the woman. She recoiled. Her hands shook as she grabbed a dish towel off the beige granite countertop and rubbed her palms against it.

"Who was that you were talking to?"

"The, um, the gas company. They wanted to know when they could come out and inspect the meter."

"And you told them that they need to figure it out for themselves?" he asked. "How does that work?"

The cameraman zoomed in on the woman's face. A thin film of perspiration covered her flushed, gaunt cheeks.

Lena's heart began to race. She covered her mouth, anxious for what was to come.

"I'm sorry, I didn't hear you," the man continued after the woman failed to respond. "I said, *how does that work?*" he repeated, his voice rising in anger. "And why would you just hang up on the customer service rep so rudely like that?"

The woman's lower lip began to quiver. Her eyes filled with tears. It was clear that she feared whoever was standing on the other side of the camera.

"I don't know," she whispered.

Lena clenched her hands together tightly. She bit the inside of her cheek as adrenaline-fueled anxiety filled her chest. The video didn't appear to be some sort of prank. Lena felt as though this woman was in real danger, and she had a sinking feeling that things weren't going to end well for her.

"I don't know!" the man mocked her in a whiny tone.

The camera suddenly moved away from the woman. It looked as though the cameraman was walking out of the room.

"Wait, is that it?" Lena muttered aloud. "It's over? What was the point of—"

She stopped midsentence when the cameraman focused on a round wooden table. There was an open laptop sitting in the middle of it.

"Wait, what is going on here?" he asked, zooming in closer.

"No," the woman whimpered. "No, *wait!*"

He aimed the camera back at her as she hurried across the room and lunged across the table. But before she could slam the laptop shut, he pulled it away from her.

"Have you been going through my stuff?" the man yelled. *"Again?"*

"No! I was, I was just looking for some—"

"Don't lie to me!" he roared. "You're still spying on me, and I'm sick of it!"

The man stormed toward her. She ran across the kitchen, screaming out in pain after banging her hip against the edge of the island's granite countertop.

"Oh no," Lena moaned, watching as the woman cowered in the corner against a pantry door.

The cameraman moved toward her, zooming in on her twisted, terrified expression. His sinister chuckle creaked through Lena's speakers. He was clearly enjoying seeing the woman in fear.

"Aw, don't cry!" he insisted, his exaggerated tone

dripping with sarcasm. "Now, tell me. Were you snooping through my computer? And did that snooping have anything to do with the call you were on just now?"

"No, no, no," the woman uttered, rapidly shaking her head from side to side. She raised her hands in the air, as if to protect herself.

"You're gonna pay for whatever it is you've done," the man growled.

Lena felt the urge to jump through her computer screen and save this helpless woman.

"*Please*," the woman mumbled, "I didn't do anything wrong."

"Oh, but your little secret phone call and my open laptop tell a different story."

The man's hand slowly inched toward the woman's throat.

"I'm gonna give you one last chance to come clean. Who were you talking to?"

"I told you. The gas co—"

Before she could finish, he wrapped his hand around her throat and squeezed tightly.

Lena screamed at the sight of his fingertips digging into her flesh.

"Stop!" the woman wheezed. "You're hurting me. I can't… I can't breathe. Come on. Stop it, Pe—"

Suddenly, the screen went black. The words *TO BE CONTINUED* appeared, then the video ended.

"Lena!" her mother called out. "You okay in there? Did I just hear you scream?"

"I'm fine! I just got startled by something I saw online."

"Okay. I'm making a pot of chili for lunch. It should be done in about an…"

Lena couldn't focus on what her mother was saying. She was too busy calling David to tell him about the video she'd just watched.

Chapter Twenty-One

David stood inside Walton's Antique Store, which was located next door to The Ocean Grill. Clemmington PD, along with LAPD, was swarming the area. They were waiting for Lena to arrive at the restaurant with undercover LAPD officer Chad Ingram.

David glanced down at his watch. It was a quarter to eight. Lena and Officer Ingram were due to arrive at eight o'clock.

David adjusted the volume on his radio adapter and pushed his Bluetooth headset farther into his ears.

"Ingram, what's your location?" he asked.

"We're heading down Berman Street now. So we should be arriving at the restaurant in about ten minutes."

"Ten-four. Lena, how are you doing? Hanging in there?"

"I am. Feeling good. And confident. I think this is it. This go-round, we're gonna catch that bastard."

"Yes, we are," David agreed, his deep voice filled with conviction.

He'd been worried that Lena would grow fearful

as they got closer to the day of the stunt. Hearing her self-assured tone was a relief.

"We're all set on this end," he continued. "The LAPD's undercover officers are tucked away inside The Ocean Grill. We're still waiting for our suspect to arrive. He was supposed to be here at seven, but he sent me a message through the *Gonna Get Got* site claiming he's driving in from LA and got caught up in traffic."

Miles, who was standing next to David, threw him a look of doubt.

"I'm thinking he's going to wait until Lena and Officer Ingram get here before he shows up," Miles said. "Just to make sure that this whole thing is legit."

"Judging by his past behavior, that does sound like something he'd do," Lena said. "Is LAPD's undercover officer Braxton in position at the front of the restaurant?"

"Yes, he is," David confirmed. "And all of the officers have their earpieces in so that we can communicate with one another. Undercover officers are wearing body cams, too, and we're livestreaming the footage. So while Clemmington PD is here at Walton's, we can see everything that's going on next door with the surveillance system we've set up."

"So it sounds like we're fully covered on all ends," Lena said.

"Absolutely. No more slipups."

David and Lena were interrupted by Officer Ingram.

"We're about three minutes away," he said. "Any sign of the suspect's arrival?"

"Not yet," Chief Scott chimed in from the restaurant. "But we're keeping a close eye out. Why don't you all stay in the car until he gets here? When he pulls up, you two can act as if you're getting out of the car. Then when he heads toward the restaurant, we'll take him down."

"Will do," Officer Ingram replied.

David turned around and wiped his damp brow as he eyed the store. The lights were low, and officers were tucked away around the perimeter of the small establishment.

They'd promised the owner that they wouldn't disturb any of his precious glass vases, lamps and statues lining the shelves. He made them swear not to go near the glass display cases that stood in the middle of the floor, which housed his fine jewelry, handbags and small heirlooms. So the officers made sure to steer clear of that area.

"We're turning the corner and heading down Roosevelt Boulevard now," Officer Ingram said. "We'll hang back by the end of the block until the suspect arrives."

"Ten-four," Chief Love said. He ducked down behind the antique store's picture window and peered through his binoculars. "I can see you coming this way. When we see the suspect's vehicle approaching, which Lena has confirmed may be a black sports car with large, spiked chrome wheels, we'll direct you to pull up in front of the restaurant."

"Copy that."

David unbuttoned the top button on his crisp white shirt. He ran his hands down the sides of his face as a strong mix of dopamine and adrenaline rushed through his system.

The temperature felt as though it was increasing by the minute. When his heart began to palpitate unsteadily, he closed his eyes and took a deep breath.

Be cool, he told himself. *Lena will be fine. This time, the plan will go off without a hitch...*

Those words ran through his mind over and over again until they were disrupted by the sound of a roaring car engine.

"That's him!" David heard Lena shriek. "That's our suspect's car. I'd recognize the sound of that engine anywhere."

David's eyes shot open. He bent down and hurried toward the window, startled by the unnerved tone in Lena's voice. Gone was the cool confidence she'd exuded just minutes before.

"Stay calm, Lena," David said soothingly, despite the fact that he was struggling to contain his own anxiety. "Everything is under control. We've got the scene completely surrounded, and there's no way that the suspect will even be able to get near you. Okay?"

"Okay," she replied, her tone slightly wavering.

David felt a throbbing pain shoot through his chest. Had he not known better, David would've thought that he was on the verge of having a heart attack. But ever since he'd begun working in law enforcement, he experienced the aching sensation whenever a big arrest was about to go down.

Take your own advice and calm down, he told himself. David looked out onto the street. He saw a black sports car slowing down, creeping toward the front of The Ocean Grill.

"Looks like our suspect has arrived," Chief Love said. "Chief Scott, Officer Braxton, are you and your team in place and ready to go?"

"Yes, sir," Chief Scott responded. "You have no idea how ready we are."

"Imagine how I feel considering this maniac is coming after my daughter. Before this is all over with, you may have to stop me from choking him to death."

David reached over and gave Chief Love a reassuring pat on the back.

"Don't worry, sir. He's going to pay for what he's done, to Lena as well as all of the other victims."

The piercing sound of screeching tires filled the air. David looked out onto the street. The suspect had stopped his car a few feet in front of the restaurant.

"All right, team," Chief Scott said. "Let's get prepared to move—"

He stopped abruptly when the suspect pulled away from the curb.

"Come on!" the chief yelled. "Where the hell is he going?"

"Do you think we should have Lena and Officer Ingram pull up to the restaurant so that the suspect will see that they're here?" David asked. "Just in case he's having second thoughts?"

"Good idea. Lena, Ingram, head toward The Ocean Grill and park right in front."

"On the way, sir," Officer Ingram responded.

David's eyes remained glued to the street. He watched as Officer Ingram drove up to the restaurant's entrance.

The suspect's vehicle came to a sudden stop, about fifty feet away from the grill. He turned off the engine. The lights went out. But he remained inside the car.

"He's not getting out," Lena said.

David could once again hear the panic in her voice. He clenched his jaws together tightly, feeling uneasy with what he was about to suggest.

"Lena, we're going to need for you to step out of the car. I think that once the perp sees you, he'll get out, and then we'll jump in. Keep in mind he won't get near you. He'll only make visual contact. Okay?"

David waited for her to reply. She remained silent.

"Lena," Chief Love said quietly, "you can do this. We're all here to protect you. We just need for you to take this one extra step, and then it'll all be over."

After several moments passed, she finally responded.

"All right. I'm ready."

David was hit by a mix of emotions. Relief, then angst, then the one that he dreaded most. Fear.

Flashbacks of the prankster pouncing on Lena in the middle of the Cucamonga Wilderness trail filled his head. He was reminded of the sheer terror he felt at the sight of her being pummeled to the ground.

That won't happen again. Heed your own words. Trust that you and your fellow officers have this situation under control.

Despite the words of encouragement, David couldn't seem to stave off the feelings of doubt.

He snapped back to attention when Lena stepped out of the car.

"I'm on the move," she said.

Her sparkling silver pumps caught David's eye. His gaze traveled up her toned calves toward her fitted, shimmering gray wrap dress. The rhinestone hoop earrings she wore complemented her outfit. Even though they were in the middle of his most intense operation to date, he couldn't help but notice how beautiful she looked.

Lena clutched her handbag tightly. David could see her hands trembling from the store window.

"Stay calm, Lena," he said. "You're doing fine. Why don't you hang back by the car. Act like you're looking for something inside your purse while we wait for the suspect to exit his vehicle."

"Got it."

As Lena rummaged around inside her handbag, David turned his attention back to the perp's car. He still hadn't gotten out.

"What is this clown doing?" Chief Love muttered, staring at the suspect's vehicle through his binoculars. "Why hasn't he exited the vehicle yet?"

No sooner had the words left his mouth than the suspect's door opened.

"Hold on," Chief Scott interrupted. "It looks like we've got movement. Team, the suspect is stepping out of the car. Everyone get in place and follow the plan. Lena, you and Officer Ingram stay put and remain preoccupied for now."

"Copy that," Officer Ingram replied.

David turned toward the perp. His rapid breathing grew shallow as the husky man climbed out of his vehicle.

The suspect was dressed in a black suit, white shirt and black bow tie. It was the exact outfit he was instructed to wear as the restaurant's maître d'. His short, shaggy brunette wig, dark sunglasses and bushy beard completely hid his identity.

"I see our suspect walking toward the restaurant," Officer Braxton said.

"Stick with the plan," Chief Scott told him. "Lena, start heading toward the grill's entrance. As soon as the suspect gets a little closer, the entire team is going to swoop in and take him down. Everybody got that?"

"Got it," Lena and the law enforcement officers replied in unison.

David turned to Chief Love. "This is it. This nightmare is finally going to be over."

"Let's hope so."

David followed the chief as he moved toward the door and hovered in the corner. Jake and Miles lined up beside them. Each of the officers drew their guns.

"The second that the LAPD initiates the takedown," Chief Love said into his earpiece, "Clemmington PD will exit the store and assist you."

David's heart was beating so forcefully that he could feel it in his throat. He leaned forward and peered out of the glass door. The suspect appeared to be taking his sweet time getting to the restaurant.

"Lena, stand down," Officer Braxton said. "I'm in

the grill's doorway now. I'm about to step out and meet the perp."

"And we'll be right behind you," Chief Scott said.

David watched as the suspect finally approached the restaurant. Lena was only a few feet away from him. Before he could approach her, Officer Braxton swung open the door. He reached out, as if to shake the killer's hand. Just when the two men made contact, David sprinted out of the store, followed by the rest of Clemmington PD.

Boom!

An ear-piercing explosion filled the air. David pressed his hands against his ears right before a blinding light impaired his vision.

David fell back against a window front. He closed his eyes, disoriented by the sudden mayhem.

"Hold on!" Chief Love yelled. "I think the perp detonated a stun grenade!"

David choked on the billowing smoke. He stumbled along the sidewalk, ignoring the ringing in his ears and flashes in his eyes.

Despite the explosion, Officer Braxton had managed to detain the suspect.

"Let's move in!" Chief Love commanded.

Clemmington PD ran over just as the LAPD swarmed the street. Organized chaos ensued when every officer approached the perp with their guns drawn.

David swooped in. Officer Braxton forced the suspect to the ground. David held the killer's legs down while Braxton forced his wrists into a pair of handcuffs.

"You have the right to remain silent," Chief Scott began. "Anything you say can and will be used against you in a court of law. You have the right to speak to an attorney…"

Once the perp's ankles had been secured in a pair of shackles, David jumped to his feet. He stood steadfast with his weapon aimed at the killer. Along with the rush of excitement he was feeling, David was overcome by a calming relief.

We got him, he thought. *We finally got him. Thanks to Lena's brilliant plan…*

David gasped and spun around. In the midst of all the commotion, he had yet to check on Lena. Now that law enforcement had the killer detained, he began searching for her. But she was nowhere in sight.

"Hey, Officer Ingram!" he called out.

"Over here!" the policeman shouted.

David looked to his right and saw him standing against the restaurant's brick wall, coughing profusely.

"Where's Lena?" David asked. "Did she go back to the car?"

Officer Ingram doubled over. "I—I think I saw her run inside the restaurant," he wheezed. "But after that explosion, I'm not sure."

David darted inside The Ocean Grill and looked around frantically.

"Lena!" he called out. "*Lena!* Are you in here?"

There was nothing but silence. He ran toward the back and checked the restrooms. They were empty.

David charged through the restaurant and rushed back outside.

"Has anyone seen Lena?" he yelled, now looking around for her father and brothers.

Miles appeared from the middle of the huddle, just as the officers pulled the killer up on his feet.

"I thought she was with Officer Ingram," he panted.

"Yeah, so did I. She must've gotten disoriented after the grenade went off and tried to get to safety."

"Well, she's gotta be around here somewhere. Did you check Ingram's car?"

"No, good idea."

David darted down the street. On the way to Officer Ingram's vehicle, something caught his eye. He stopped abruptly.

There, on the edge of the cracked beige concrete, was a rhinestone hoop earring.

David gagged as he tried to take in a breath of air. A feeling of dread crept up his back. He turned around and ran back toward the group of law enforcement.

"Hold on!" he called out as Chief Scott and his team escorted the killer to a police cruiser.

The men paused. David approached the suspect. He looked closely at his chubby jawline. Traces of dried white glue lined the edges of his beard. David ripped it off.

"Ouch!" the perp exclaimed.

Without saying a word, David grabbed his black aviator sunglasses and snatched them off his face.

"Hey, what's up, Corporal?" the suspect exclaimed. "So we meet again. I hope I don't get arrested for real this time. It wasn't illegal for me to take on another prank job, was it?"

David felt his lungs constrict. His chest tightened as the air around him seemingly dissipated. He opened his mouth to speak but couldn't utter a word. Because there, standing in front of him, was Christopher Ware. The prankster from the Cucamonga Wilderness trail.

Chapter Twenty-Two

Lena was sprawled out in the back seat of a car. She'd been blindfolded, and her hands were bound behind her back with duct tape.

"I can't believe you people thought I was that damn stupid," she heard her kidnapper mutter. "I mean, seriously, if I was dumb enough to fall for this setup, do you really think I would've gotten away with all of these murders?"

Lena whimpered, her eyes stinging from a mix of tears and perspiration.

"Hey!" the kidnapper yelled. "I'm talking to you!"

"We—I—I don't know!" she stammered.

She shivered at the sound of the killer's sinister chuckle.

"I don't *knooow*!" he repeated, his tone emulating hers. "Well, let me tell you what *I* know. I know that you and your little inadequate cohorts made the biggest mistake of your lives tonight."

Lena bit her bottom lip, struggling to stifle the sobs that were creeping up her throat. She was determined not to show any signs of fear, despite the fact that she was completely terrified.

How the hell did I even get here? she thought to herself.

But once she'd regained her senses after the explosion, Lena remembered.

Back when they were at the restaurant, Officer Ingram was working overtime to protect her. He'd assured Lena that he had her back. Then the grenade detonated. She and the officer were separated. Lena was left standing on the sidewalk, alone.

She'd temporarily lost her sense of sight and sound. Once she came to, an officer dressed in black LAPD tactical gear appeared from a nearby alleyway and jogged over to her.

"Lena!" he said. "We got him! Are you okay?"

"I'm fine," she replied, her eyes squinting as she tried to peer through the tinted visor on his helmet. "I'm sorry, but I can't see very well out here. Could you please tell me who you—"

She was interrupted when one of the arresting officers shouted loudly.

"I said stay down and keep your hands where I can see them!"

The policeman who'd been speaking to Lena gently wrapped his arm around her.

"Oh no," he'd moaned. "The killer seems to be giving law enforcement a hard time. Come on. Let's get you to safety. I'll take you inside the restaurant through the back door so that you won't have to go near him."

"Thank you so much." Lena sighed.

She allowed the man to lead her through the alley-way. Once they'd reached The Ocean Grill, she made a right turn and headed toward the door.

"Wrong way," the man grunted before grabbing Lena's arm and shoving her inside an unmarked black sedan.

He'd moved so fast that she hadn't had a chance to fight back, or even scream. He snatched the earpiece out of her ears and the radio adapter from her hand. Before Lena knew it, she'd been bound and blindfolded. Within seconds, the killer was speeding down the alley.

And now here she was, alone, at the killer's whim, and undoubtedly on her way to being murdered.

"Oh, look!" the killer said. "Your cell phone! Well, let's disable this thing right now just in case your little boyfriend David is trying to track your whereabouts."

Dammit! Lena thought, so out of sorts that she hadn't even realized he'd confiscated her purse.

"You know," he continued, "I'll admit, that was a slick little attempt you made to try and trap me by submitting a prank request through my website. I was actually shocked when I saw your photo. And that price tag? There's no way I was gonna turn down two thousand dollars. But then my sixth sense kicked in. I thought to myself, *self, something is amiss here...*"

Lena forced herself to stop panting. She focused on the man's voice. It sounded eerily familiar.

"I bet you're wondering where we're going," he continued before cackling wickedly, then snorting. "Don't worry. You'll soon find out."

Lena assumed he was taking her to the Cucamonga

Wilderness trail. That seemed like something he'd do; finish what he'd started in the same place where it had all begun. In his warped mind, he'd deem it poetic justice. She just hoped that David would somehow figure out a way to find her.

DAVID SHOVED CHRISTOPHER and pushed through the crowd of police officers.

"Get him the hell away from me!" he yelled. "Ingram!"

"He's over here," Chief Scott said.

David saw Officer Ingram standing against the side of the restaurant, staring down at his black leather cap-toe shoes. His hands were shoved deep inside his pockets, and his distorted expression was riddled with regret. Chief Love, Miles and Jake were surrounding him with their arms crossed.

Ingram appeared remorseful for letting Lena out of his sight. And David knew his mishap wasn't intentional. Nevertheless, he was in no mood to console him.

"Dude!" he hollered, storming over to the group. "What the *fu*—"

"*Detective*," Chief Love interrupted, pressing his hand against David's chest, "please. The man feels bad enough. We're working to retrace his and Lena's steps so that we can track her down. So let's be respectful."

"Yes, *let's*," Officer Ingram interjected, shooting David a death stare.

David pushed past the chief and swung his arm

back. Right before his fist connected with the policeman's jaw, Miles grabbed David and pulled him away.

"All right, let's go," Miles insisted, leading him down the street. "Let's walk it off."

"Walk it off? We need to go and find Lena!"

"That's what we're working on. The LAPD has already sent out several squad cars to search for her. Jake and I have been trying to track her cell phone, but it looks like it's been turned off."

"Has anybody tried to contact her cell phone carrier?" David asked.

"Officer Braxton put in a call to the LAPD's digital forensics expert. He's on it."

"Good." David dug his fingertips into his forehead and began pacing the sidewalk. "I cannot believe that idiot let Lena out of his sight. And I never should have let her talk me into this…this *prank*. The killer has been ten steps ahead of us the entire time. I don't know why I thought this time would be any different. And now, he's got my girl. I—I can't…"

David's voice broke. He bent down and pressed his hands against his knees, barely able to take in any air.

"Listen," Miles said, "we're going to find her. Believe me, I'm worried, too. But I'm trying to keep it together for the sake of you and my family."

Just as David felt Miles's hand on his shoulder, he shot straight up.

Miles jumped back, seemingly startled by the sudden move. "*Whoa.* Are you okay?"

David reached inside his back pocket and grabbed his cell phone.

"Did you happen to notice whether or not Lena was wearing her smart watch?" he asked, his eyes peeled to the phone screen.

"No, I didn't. Why?"

"Because she's got a GPS tracking system on it. If the killer has her, I'm assuming he confiscated her phone and turned it off so that we wouldn't be able to track her. But if she's wearing her smart watch, I might still be able to trace her whereabouts."

"Knowing Lena, she's got it on," Miles replied as he peered over David's shoulder. "And if that maniac does have her, hopefully she'll be able to keep it hidden from him."

"Let's hope so."

David pulled up a map on his phone. He tapped on the location services prompt and clicked Lena's name.

David held his breath, waiting to see if the green locator marker would appear.

Come on, Lena. Show me where you are...

"Anything showing up yet?" Miles asked.

"Not yet."

Just as David was hit with a sinking feeling, a green tab popped up on the map. He was so shocked that he almost dropped the phone.

"We've got movement!" he yelled.

"Where?" Miles asked frantically. "Where is she?"

David followed the white arrow guiding the green marker.

"Looks like she's heading toward Clemmington," he replied before taking off running. "I'm going to find her. I'll call you from the car for backup!"

Chapter Twenty-Three

Lena winced in pain as gritty dirt scraped against the bottoms of her bare feet. She stumbled forward, expecting to fall flat on her face until she was abruptly pulled back up.

"Come on!" the killer growled. "You know how to hike these cliffs. You should be a pro by now. Stay on your feet before I throw you over the edge."

Stay strong, Lena told herself, wishing she could peek over the top of her blindfold. *Do not show fear. Do not shed another tear...*

But despite the words of encouragement, feelings of doubt and hopelessness numbed her entire body.

This is really it. I'm going to die this time.

Lena was struggling to figure out where they were. She'd tried her best to move the blindfold by rubbing the side of her face along the back seat of the car. But it'd been tied so tightly that the blindfold had not budged.

The killer hadn't driven long enough for them to be in LA's Cucamonga Wilderness. Lena wondered whether he'd taken her to a new trail, where no one would think to look for her.

"Let's *go*!" her kidnapper insisted. He yanked her arm and pulled her forward. "Someone's waiting on us. And I can't *wait* for you two to meet."

Just as he emitted another one of his sinister laughs, Lena heard a woman scream in the distance.

What the...?

"There she is!" the man exclaimed. "That's her way of greeting you, Lena. Hey! Let's play a game. Good news and bad news. Which do you want first?"

Before Lena could respond, she felt a sharp rock cut into the ball of her right foot.

"Ouch!" she shrieked, once again tumbling forward.

Stinging pain shot up her leg. When the bottom of her foot grew damp, Lena knew she was bleeding. She cried out as grainy bits of earth crept into the fresh wound.

The killer appeared oblivious to her agony.

"I said, good news or bad news!" he repeated, his gruff tone growing more impatient.

Ignore the pain, Lena thought. *Mind over matter. Mind over matter...*

"The good news," she mumbled through clenched teeth.

"All right, cool. So, the good news is, you won't have to die alone."

"Help me!" Lena heard the woman yell. *"Help!"*

Between the sound of her pleas, the killer's threats and her injured foot, Lena felt as though her limbs might give out. But she refused to collapse underneath the weight of the situation.

"Shut up!" the kidnapper hollered into the distance. "Quit being so damn impatient. We're coming!"

The man stopped. Lena felt him lean against her, his hot, stale breath singeing the side of her face. When the tip of his cold nose brushed against her earlobe, she cringed, but kept her composure.

"And now," he murmured, "the bad news. You *are* going to die. Now, let's go!"

Lena gasped as the man grabbed her legs, picked her up and threw her over his shoulder. She lost her breath while he ran full speed ahead. She bounced around wildly, almost falling several times. Lena held on by gripping the back of his jacket so tightly that her fingernails bent against the rough fabric.

The woman's screams grew louder. Which meant they were getting closer to her.

"Jan!" the man yelled. "Shut the hell up!"

When the woman screamed again, Lena heard a loud slap. And then, quiet whimpering.

Please God, Lena thought, *help me…*

"Okay, ladies," the man said. "This is the moment of truth. Are you ready?"

Neither of the women replied.

"I said, are you ready!" he hollered.

"Yes," they responded in distraught unison.

"All right, then. Here we go. Three, two, one. *Ta-da!*"

Lena squealed when she felt the man's grubby fingers grab the blindfold and rip it from around her head. She blinked rapidly, struggling to adjust her vision.

He shined a flashlight in her face. He then aimed it at a woman standing across from her.

Lena was horrified when she realized that the woman was tied to a tree. Her pale green eyes were drenched and swollen. And her long blond hair was stuck to her sweaty face and neck.

Lena froze. She took a closer look at the woman. For some strange reason, she looked familiar. The eyes, the hair…

The name Jan.

And that's when it hit Lena. The woman standing in front of her was the same person in the Disloyalty video on the *Gonna Get Got* website.

"Lena," the man began.

She turned to the killer, hoping to finally get a good look at him. But he was still wearing his tactical helmet.

"Meet Jan," he continued. "Jan, meet Lena. Now, technically, you two have already met. Because when Jan here overstepped her bounds by meddling in my business and finding my website, she had the nerve to call *you*, Lena, and drop a dime on me. Can you believe that? And what's worse, I had to choke the hell out of the bitch just to get her to admit it!"

As his voice grew louder, Jan writhed against the tree. She emitted a guttural howl.

"Didn't I tell you to shut up!" he yelled.

Lena expected him to go after Jan. But instead he lunged at her.

The killer grabbed Lena by the collar and shoved her against the tree. He leaned in and pressed his face against hers.

"You're probably wondering who this snitch is to me," he said, sneering. "Believe it or not, she's my *wife*. But not for long. Because in the next few minutes, she'll be a beautiful corpse, and I'll be a grieving widower. And as you for, Lena Love, you'll soon be nothing but a dead forensic investigator who failed to capture one of California's most prolific serial killers."

The man reached out and tucked several strands of Lena's hair behind her ear. Her chin trembled in disgust. She felt the urge to kick him in the groin.

That urge quickly subsided when he pulled a knife out of his back pocket.

Lena pressed her body farther into the tree. Its bark tore at her dress's thin silk material, scraping against her skin. Her foot throbbed uncontrollably. But she was so focused on the knife's long, sharp blade that she barely felt any pain.

"How are we going to get out of this?" Jan whispered to her. "I don't wanna die!"

Lena glanced over at the man. He slowly pointed the knife at her. She could hear his heavy panting. A slight moan rumbled when he exhaled. Bile crept up her throat as she sensed his excitement.

The blade of the knife grazed Lena's neckline. Jan screamed out.

"Help. *Help!*"

"I thought I told you to shut up!" the man yelled.

He swung the knife in Jan's direction. When she

cried out, Lena glanced over at her. She was horrified to see that the man had slashed her cheek. Blood gushed from the gash and streamed down her neck.

"Your *throat* is gonna be next!" he told her.

The killer grabbed Jan's collar and tore at her blouse. Buttons went flying everywhere.

"Why are you *doing* this?" she sputtered. "You're insane!"

Lena tightened her lips, intent on suppressing the scream rumbling in the back of her throat.

The man tapped the tip of the knife against Jan's chin. She closed her eyes as her lower lip quivered. He dragged the blade down her neck, ignoring the blood that was dripping down her chest. When he pressed the knife into her flesh, she screamed out in pain.

"Stop it!" Lena couldn't help but yell.

"Stay out of this!" he demanded, reaching out and grabbing her neck. He squeezed tightly, then pushed her back.

Lena stumbled and fell against the side of the tree. Sharp-edged twigs sliced into her bare soles. She grunted loudly, fighting the pain while somehow managing to stay on her feet.

"You see this, Lena?" the killer barked.

She glanced wearily over at him. He was shining his flashlight directly at Jan. When he pointed the knife above her left breast, Lena saw that a heart had been carved into her chest.

"Aaah!" she shrieked before spinning around and taking off running.

Adrenaline numbed the pain in her feet. She ran

as fast as she could, praying that she could somehow get away.

But just as she laid eyes on the hiking trail up ahead, Lena felt the kidnapper's hand on the back of her head. He grabbed a handful of hair, gripping it tightly while pulling her back.

She fell to the ground. But that didn't stop him. Despite her kicking and flailing, he dragged her across the ground like a rag doll. When they reached the tree, he yanked her back up onto her feet and shoved her hard against the trunk.

"Try that again," he growled, "and I'll stab you right in the heart."

Lena's entire body trembled uncontrollably. She was stunned by the sinister evil standing before her. And she knew that if law enforcement didn't arrive soon, both she and Jan would be killed.

Please, David, please come and find us...

Chapter Twenty-Four

"I've got Lena's exact location," David said to Miles, who he'd been talking to from the car. "Her watch is pinging near the Juniper hiking trail. Get here with backup. *Now!*"

"We're on our way!"

David disconnected the call and flew down the street. He pulled over in front of the trail's entrance so fast that his car jumped the curb.

David barely turned the engine off before he hopped out. He grabbed his Glock 22 from its holster and held it close before charging up the trail. When he heard a loud scream in the distance, David quickened his pace.

It didn't take long for him to reach the outskirts of the crime scene. He used the light from his cell phone to guide his footsteps. David ducked down and moved in swiftly, but carefully.

Within minutes, he noticed Lena leaning against a tree, next to a woman he didn't recognize. The killer was standing in front of the woman with what appeared to be his hand wrapped around her throat. He was dressed in all black and barely visible. But the

flashlight he was holding shined a beam of brightness in the vicinity.

As he moved in closer, David let out a sigh of relief. While Lena was far from being out of danger, at
least she was still alive.

"Get down on your knees," he heard the killer yell.
"Both of you!"

The man untied the rope binding the other woman to
the tree. His head dropped down toward the ground as
he watched the two women follow his command. David
heard him cackle loudly as they knelt in front of him.

When the killer placed his hands underneath their
chins and jerked their faces upward, David moved in
closer. He cocked his gun and stayed low. The sight
of a knife in the man's hands forced him to increase
his speed.

Just as he approached the group, the sound of blar-
ing sirens filled the air.

"What the...?" the killer said.

David ran toward him at full speed with his gun
aimed at his chest.

"Police! Freeze!" David yelled. "Drop your weapon
and get your hands up!"

The man slowly backed away from the women.
Lena grabbed the other woman and pulled her to safety.

The killer was still moving away from David with
the knife in his hand.

"Stop right where you are!" David ordered. "Drop
the weapon and get your hands up. *Now!*"

"Yes, *sir*!" the suspect yelled, right before he jetted
off into the woods.

"David!" Lena screamed. "Don't let him get away!"

"I won't!" David assured her as he started to run.

He aimed his gun at the killer, shot and missed.

"Dammit!"

The suspect bobbed and wove in between the trees. David shot again. The bullet ricocheted off a tree trunk and disappeared into the brush.

The killer was getting away. He appeared to know the wooded area well.

David increased his speed, ignoring the rough foliage scraping against his legs. When he heard a loud grunt and thud up ahead, he shined his cell phone's light in the distance.

The suspect had tripped over a thick branch and fallen to the ground.

"Freeze!" David yelled. "Stay down!"

He hurried over to the man, shoving his phone inside his pocket and pulling out his handcuffs, then securing his gun inside its holster.

"Ooow," the killer moaned. "I'm injured. I think I broke my leg…"

David ignored him. He was too busy grabbing his wrists. Just as David went to apply the handcuffs, the suspect quickly rolled over and kicked him in the groin.

"Ahh!" David yelled.

He fell over onto his back. The nauseating sting was excruciating. But when the killer tried to jump up and run off, David kicked out his leg. He hooked his right foot underneath the man's left calf.

The killer tumbled to the ground.

David fought through the pain shooting up his abdomen and sat up. As soon as he did, the suspect reached over and punched him in the jaw. Both men struggled to get to their feet. David made it up first. He hit the man with a swift uppercut to the chin, then unholstered and pointed his gun.

"If you make one more move," David huffed, "I will shoot you. And this time, I won't miss."

The killer slumped his shoulders in defeat.

"Detective Hudson!" David heard Miles call out. "Where are you?"

"Over here!"

The policeman ran up and quickly handcuffed the suspect.

The Clemmington PD and LAPD came rushing over. The women weren't far behind them.

When the law enforcement officers saw that David had finally caught the killer, they gave him a round of applause. Lena walked to the front of the group, clapping the loudest.

"I want you to remove that helmet," she said to David. "I've been waiting for a long time to finally see this man's disgusting face."

"It would be my pleasure," David said.

When he pulled off the helmet, Lena moved in and squinted her eyes, then gasped. She jumped back, covering her mouth in shock.

"Peter?" she uttered. "Peter Ballentine?"

"Wait, you know him?" David asked.

"I—I do. We went to Pacific Western University together. We were both studying to become forensic investigators."

Miles stepped forward, shaking his head from side to side. "Wait, this is Peter Ballentine? *The* Peter Ballentine? The guy who was always competing with you? And losing?"

Peter squared his shoulders and held his head high. "Yes. That's me. *The* Peter Ballentine. And Lena may have won in the classroom. And gotten the job with the LAPD over me. But look at all the damage I've done to her. How good could she possibly be at her job, considering how long it took for you all to catch me? It took not one, but two police forces to take me down. *Two*. Ha!"

"All right," David said, gripping Peter's arm. "That's enough. We're taking you down to the station."

David noticed Lena's chest heaving up and down, as if she was struggling to catch her breath. Her father and brothers stood around her, offering up words of support.

Just as David stopped to check on her, Chief Scott stepped in.

"Detective Hudson," he said, "why don't you stay here and look after Lena? We can take the suspect into custody. And we'll make sure the other victim gets the medical attention that she needs, too. Lena," he continued, turning toward her, "are you sure you don't want to go to the hospital?"

"No. I'm fine," she said confidently. "I've got a few cuts and bruises, but I can treat them myself. Just get Jan to the hospital."

"We will. And I'll check back in with you and Detective Hudson shortly."

David nodded his head. "Thank you, sir."

Chief Scott and several members of the LAPD took hold of Peter. Before they walked away, Peter glanced back at Lena.

"You obviously aren't as great as everyone thinks you are!" he ranted. "And your investigative skills *suck*. Too bad my killing spree single-handedly ruined your entire career..."

His voice faded off as the officers dragged him toward the trail.

Lena's father and brothers encircled her in a Love family embrace. It appeared as though she hadn't heard a word that the killer had spoken.

"This horrid ordeal is finally over, baby," Chief Love told her. "Now you can move on from it and get back to living your life. Hopefully back here in Clemmington."

"Dad," Miles interjected. "Really? After all that Lena's been through? At least let her recuperate before you start trying to get her to come back home."

"You're right, son. I'm just glad that my girl is okay."

Chief Love turned to David and shook his hand firmly. "Excellent work, Detective. Without you, we may have had a very different outcome."

"How did you even find me?" Lena asked him.

"Your smart watch. I tracked down your location through it."

Lena reached down and grabbed her wrist. The watch had been covered by her sleeve.

"Oh my... I forgot that I was even wearing it. Thank

you!" she exclaimed, rushing over and throwing her arms around him.

As he embraced her tightly, Lena's father and brothers gave him a thumbs-up, then walked off.

"I'm so glad you're okay," David said, his voice muffled within her wild curls. "And I am so sorry that tonight didn't go as planned."

"If anybody should be apologizing, it's me. Remember, this whole prank thing was my idea."

David slowly pulled away from Lena, his hands sliding down the sides of her waist before resting on her hips.

"Well," he said, "the bottom line is, it worked. Our suspect is in custody, you're okay and we saved another victim's life tonight. I didn't even get a chance to ask her name, or how she was kidnapped."

"Her name is Jan, and she's Peter's wife. She's also the woman who called me anonymously and told me about the *Gonna Get Got* website. Oh! And that was her in the video I was telling you about, where a woman was being confronted by an unseen man. Peter actually filmed it while she and I were on the phone."

"*Really?* Wow. You and I have got a lot to catch up on."

"Yes, we do. It'll all come out once we get to the station."

David glanced down at her feet, noticing that her shoes had been replaced with a pair of booties. The blue fabric was stained with blood.

"Wait," he said, "what happened to your shoes? And your *feet*?"

"My shoes got lost in the midst of the kidnapping. As a result, my poor feet paid the price."

"Well, we can't have that, now, can we?" David asked before picking her up and carrying her back down the trail.

Lena wrapped her arms around his neck.

"Thank you for coming to my rescue," she whispered.

"You're welcome. Thank you for being one of the strongest people I know," he replied before softly kissing her lips.

Chapter Twenty-Five

Lena and David were sitting out on her parents' deck, enjoying the tranquil sunset.

She leaned back in her lawn chair and took another sip of wine, then turned to him and smiled. When he held out his hand, she reached over and interlaced her fingers within his.

"I still can't believe that this nightmare is over," he said. "But I'm sure no one is happier about it than you."

"*I* still can't believe that Peter Ballentine is the one who committed all of those murders, just to spite me."

"Yeah, what was his beef with you anyway?"

"Well, as you know, I graduated top of my class in college. Year after year, Peter would always try to outdo me. It never worked, and he always came in second. Sometimes third. And he was a smart guy. But he was just...*strange*. And antisocial. Bottom line, he just didn't have *it*. And he resented me, because according to our professors, I did."

"Of course you did," David murmured. "As a matter of fact, you still do."

Lena's eyes lowered as she tucked her hair behind her ears.

"Thank you. So anyway, the competition between Peter and me really came to a head right before graduation. We both applied for forensic science positions with the LAPD. I got hired and he didn't. Peter was livid."

"Oh, I bet he was."

"Then he really lost it when he found out I'd earned a certificate in crime scene investigation, which gave me an edge during the hiring process. He even showed up at my graduation party uninvited, drunk, and dressed in a pair of plaid pajamas. After giving the most bizarre congratulatory speech ever, saying that the streets of LA would probably eat me alive, he stormed out."

"*Wow.* And he ended up being the one to try and take you down. What a coward. You should've seen how smug he was in that interrogation room when he confessed to the crimes. But as hard as he tried to get away with it and turn you into another victim, he failed. And you won. *Again.*"

"Exactly." Lena crossed her legs and shifted in her chair so that she was facing David. "That's what this was all about. And with that being said, thank you for those kind compliments."

"You're welcome. Just speaking the truth." David ran his thumb along the top of her hand. "I'm just glad you're safe now, he's behind bars, and you can live your life again without fear."

"Cheers to that," she replied, reaching over and clinking her glass against his.

"Speaking of living your life again, what are your plans? Do you think you'll be going to LA and getting back to work soon?"

Lena could hear the strain in his voice. She peered over at him. He stared back at her, his eyelids lowered. He raised his head off the back of the chair, seemingly anxious to hear her response.

"We'll see," she replied coyly. "My father did offer me a pretty lucrative position here with the Clemmington PD."

"Did he really?"

"Yep. He did."

David moved his chair closer to hers.

"And what'd you say?" he asked.

"I told him that I'd need some time to think about it. And that he'd have to meet a few of my demands in order for me to consider it."

"What exactly do those demands entail?"

"Well, for starters, I wouldn't want to be running back and forth between the police station and the crime lab. So he'd have to build some sort of lab for me here in town. And if the cost is a deterrent, I told him I'd be willing to share it with a few of the neighboring towns, as long as they'd contribute to the budget."

David nodded his head. "That sounds reasonable. How did he respond?"

Lena threw her head back and laughed. "Pretty favorably, actually. He said, and I quote, 'I'd build you a lab, a house, a car *and* a boat if that's what it would take to bring my baby girl back to Clemmington.'"

"Oh, wow. How could you say no to that?"

She turned to him and smiled. "I couldn't. So I didn't."

David shot straight up in his chair. "Wait, so does that mean you're moving back home?"

"Yes, it does."

He jumped up, pulled Lena out of her chair, wrapped her in his arms and twirled her around the deck.

"David!" she squealed. "What are you doing?"

"What does it look like I'm doing? I'm celebrating!"

She pressed her lips against his neck while embracing him tightly. When he slowed down, she held his head in her hands.

"Looks like I'm finally gonna get my girl back," he murmured as they gazed at one another.

"Looks to me like you already did."

"So when are we going to LA to pack up your things?"

"How does tomorrow sound?"

"Tomorrow sounds perfect," David replied before leaning in and kissing her passionately.

* * * * *

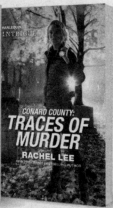

#2079 SHERIFF IN THE SADDLE
The Law in Lubbock County • by Delores Fossen
The town wants her to arrest her former boyfriend, bad boy Cullen Brodie, for a murder on his ranch—but Sheriff Leigh Mercer has no evidence and refuses. The search for the killer draws them passionately close again...and into relentless danger. Not only could Leigh lose her job for not collaring Brodie...but they could both lose their lives.

#2080 ALPHA TRACKER
K-9s on Patrol • by Cindi Myers
After lawman Dillon Diaz spent one incredible weekend with the mysterious Roslyn Kern, he's shocked to encounter her months later when he's assigned to rescue an injured hiker in the mountains. Now, battling a fiery blaze and an escaped fugitive, it's up to Dillon and his K-9, Bentley, to protect long-lost Rosie—and Dillon's unborn child.

#2081 EYEWITNESS MAN AND WIFE
A Ree and Quint Novel • by Barb Han
Relentless ATF agent Quint Casey won't let his best lead die with a murdered perp. He and his undercover wife, Agent Ree Sheppard, must secretly home in on a powerful weapons kingpin. But their undeniable attraction is breaking too many rules for them to play this mission safe—or guarantee their survival...

#2082 CLOSING IN ON THE COWBOY
Kings of Coyote Creek • by Carla Cassidy
Rancher Johnny King thought he'd moved on since Chelsea Black broke their engagement and shattered his heart. But with his emotions still raw following his father's murder, Chelsea's return to town and vulnerability touches Johnny's heart. And when a mysterious stalker threatens Chelsea's life, protecting her means risking his heart again for the woman who abandoned him.

#2083 RETRACING THE INVESTIGATION
The Saving Kelby Creek Series • by Tyler Anne Snell
When Sheriff Jones Murphy rescues his daughter and her teacher, the widower is surprised to encounter Cassandra West again—and there's no mistaking she's pregnant. Now someone wants her dead for unleashing a secret that stunned their town. And though his heart is closed, Jones's sense of duty isn't letting anyone hurt what is his.

#2084 CANYON CRIME SCENE
The Lost Girls • by Carol Ericson
Cade Larson needs LAPD fingerprint expert Lori Del Valle's help tracking down his troubled sister. And when fingerprints link Cade's sister to another missing woman—and a potentially nefarious treatment center—Lori volunteers to go undercover. Will their dangerous plan bring a predator to justice or tragically end their reunion?

"CHELSEA, WHAT'S GOING ON?" Johnny clutched his cell
phone to his ear and at the same time he sat up and turned
on the lamp on his nightstand.

"That man…that man is here. He tried to b-break in."
The words came amid sobs. "He…he was at my back
d-door and breaking the gl-glass to get in."

"Hang up and call Lane," he instructed as he got out
of bed.

"I…already called, but n-nobody is here yet."

Johnny could hear the abject terror in her voice, and an
icy fear shot through him. "Where are you now?"

"I'm in the kitchen."

"Get to the bathroom and lock yourself in. Do you hear me? Lock yourself in the bathroom, and I'll be there as quickly as I can," he instructed.

"Please hurry. I don't know where he is now, and I'm so scared."

"Just get to the bathroom. Lock the door and don't open it for anyone but me or the police." He hung up and quickly dressed. He then strapped on his gun and left his cabin. Any residual sleepiness he might have felt was instantly gone, replaced by a sharp edge of tension that tightened his chest.

Don't miss
Closing in on the Cowboy *by Carla Cassidy,*
available July 2022 wherever
Harlequin Intrigue books and ebooks are sold.

Harlequin.com

Get 4 FREE REWARDS!

We'll send you 2 FREE Books plus 2 FREE Mystery Gifts.

FREE Value Over $20

Both the **Harlequin Intrigue®** and **Harlequin® Romantic Suspense** series feature compelling novels filled with heart-racing action-packed romance that will keep you on the edge of your seat.

YES! Please send me 2 FREE novels from the Harlequin Intrigue or Harlequin Romantic Suspense series and my 2 FREE gifts (gifts are worth about $10 retail). After receiving them, if I don't wish to receive any more books, I can return the shipping statement marked "cancel." If I don't cancel, I will receive 6 brand-new Harlequin Intrigue Larger-Print books every month and be billed just $5.99 each in the U.S. or $6.49 each in Canada, a savings of at least 14% off the cover price or 4 brand-new Harlequin Romantic Suspense books every month and be billed just $4.99 each in the U.S. or $5.74 each in Canada, a savings of at least 13% off the cover price. It's quite a bargain! Shipping and handling is just 50¢ per book in the U.S. and $1.25 per book in Canada.* I understand that accepting the 2 free books and gifts places me under no obligation to buy anything. I can always return a shipment and cancel at any time. The free books and gifts are mine to keep no matter what I decide.

Choose one: ☐ **Harlequin Intrigue Larger-Print** (199/399 HDN GNXC) ☐ **Harlequin Romantic Suspense** (240/340 HDN GNMZ)

Name (please print)

Address   Apt. #

City   State/Province   Zip/Postal Code

Email: Please check this box ☐ if you would like to receive newsletters and promotional emails from Harlequin Enterprises ULC and its affiliates. You can unsubscribe anytime.

Mail to the Harlequin Reader Service:
IN U.S.A.: P.O. Box 1341, Buffalo, NY 14240-8531
IN CANADA: P.O. Box 603, Fort Erie, Ontario L2A 5X3

Want to try 2 free books from another series! Call 1-800-873-8635 or visit www.ReaderService.com.

*Terms and prices subject to change without notice. Prices do not include sales taxes, which will be charged (if applicable) based on your state or country of residence. Canadian residents will be charged applicable taxes. Offer not valid in Quebec. This offer is limited to one order per household. Books received may not be as shown. Not valid for current subscribers to the Harlequin Intrigue or Harlequin Romantic Suspense series. All orders subject to approval. Credit or debit balances in a customer's account(s) may be offset by any other outstanding balance owed by or to the customer. Please allow 4 to 6 weeks for delivery. Offer available while quantities last.

Your Privacy—Your information is being collected by Harlequin Enterprises ULC, operating as Harlequin Reader Service. For a complete summary of the information we collect, how we use this information and to whom it is disclosed, please visit our privacy notice located at corporate.harlequin.com/privacy-notice. From time to time we may also exchange your personal information with reputable third parties. If you wish to opt out of this sharing of your personal information, please visit readerservice.com/consumerschoice or call 1-800-873-8635. **Notice to California Residents**—Under California law, you have specific rights to control and access your data. For more information on these rights and how to exercise them, visit corporate.harlequin.com/california-privacy.

HIHRS22

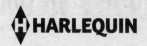
HARLEQUIN

Heartfelt or thrilling, passionate or uplifting—Harlequin is more than just happily-ever-after.

With twelve different series to choose from and new books available every month, you are sure to find stories that will move you, uplift you, inspire and delight you.

Love Harlequin romance?

DISCOVER.

Be the first to find out about promotions,
news and exclusive content!

f Facebook.com/HarlequinBooks

y Twitter.com/HarlequinBooks

O Instagram.com/HarlequinBooks

P Pinterest.com/HarlequinBooks

You Tube YouTube.com/HarlequinBooks

ReaderService.com

EXPLORE.

Sign up for the Harlequin e-newsletter and
download a free book from any series at
TryHarlequin.com

CONNECT.

Join our Harlequin community to
share your thoughts and connect
with other romance readers!
Facebook.com/groups/HarlequinConnection

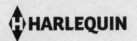